2024

MSA

Mittlerer Schulabschluss

Schleswig-Holstein

Englisch

LÖSUNGEN

STARK

11. ergänzte Auflage
www.stark-verlag.de

Inhalt

Sobald die Prüfungsaufgaben 2023 freigegeben sind, kannst du die dazugehörigen Lösungen als PDF auf der Plattform MyStark herunterladen (Zugangscode vgl. Umschlaginnenseite).

Autorinnen und Autoren der Lösungen:

- Lösungen zu Hörverstehen, Leseverstehen, Schreiben:
  Paul Jenkinson, Frank Lemke, Kathryn Nussdorf, Wencke Sockolowsky, Christina Wolkenhauer
- Lösungen zu Sprechen / Mediation:
  Sabine Frost, Bina Holdmann, Babett Neumann
- Lösungen zu den Original-Prüfungsaufgaben:
  2019–2021: Melanie Thol, ab 2022: Jenny Börke

Vorwort

Liebe Schülerin, lieber Schüler,

dies ist der Lösungsband zum Buch *Mittlerer Schulabschluss Schleswig-Holstein Englisch* (Bestellnummer D01150). Er enthält ausführliche und kommentierte Lösungsvorschläge zu den Übungsaufgaben und zu den Original-Prüfungsaufgaben ab 2019.

Die Lösungen ermöglichen es dir, deine Leistung einzuschätzen. Es handelt sich um **Lösungsvorschläge**, die dir zeigen, wie man die Aufgaben richtig und umfassend beantworten kann. Das heißt, dass – außer bei sogenannten geschlossenen Aufgaben wie *Multiple Choice* oder *True/False* – auch andere Lösungen als die hier abgedruckten möglich sind. Die Lösungen sind manchmal recht ausführlich und geben dir Anregungen, was du alles schreiben könntest. Deine Antworten müssen aber nicht immer so lang sein. Wichtig ist, dass du die Hinweise beachtest, die in der Aufgabenstellung genannt sind, und alles **vollständig** und **möglichst fehlerfrei** bearbeitest.

Außerdem gilt: Versuche, die Aufgabe zunächst **selbstständig** zu lösen, und sieh nicht gleich in der Lösung nach. Solltest du nicht weiterkommen, helfen dir die grau markierten **Hinweise und Tipps** vor der jeweiligen Lösung. Arbeite unbedingt selbstständig weiter, nachdem du sie gelesen hast. Vergleiche erst am Schluss deine Lösung mit der hier angebotenen Lösung und kontrolliere deine eigenen Ergebnisse. Lies zu allen Aufgaben, die du nicht richtig lösen konntest oder bei denen du dir unsicher warst, noch einmal die allgemeinen Erläuterungen in dem entsprechenden Kapitel im Trainingsband.

Viel Spaß beim Üben und vor allem viel Erfolg in der Prüfung!

▶ Lösungen zum Kompetenzbereich Hörverstehen

✎ *Allgemeiner Hinweis: Zum Lösen aller Aufgaben im Kapitel Hörverstehen solltest du dir den jeweiligen Text, wie in der Prüfung, zunächst zweimal genau anhören. Für die „additional tasks" kannst du den Hörtext natürlich noch öfter hören. Sie dienen als zusätzliche Übungsmöglichkeit. Lies den Hörverstehenstext nur, wenn du mit den Lösungen ganz unsicher bist und gar nicht weiterkommst.*

Listening Test 1: How may I help you, madam?

1. ✎ *Hinweis: Bei dieser Aufgabe musst du die Tabelle mit Informationen aus dem Gespräch zwischen Ms Lawson und Mike Murphy, dem Reisebüroangestellten, vervollständigen. Du bekommst dadurch einen Überblick über den Text und eine Hilfe für die anschließende Aufgabe.*

reason for the call	destination	name of the travel agent	travel partner
a holiday booking / a hotel reservation	Nice / France	Mike (Murphy)	Humphrey (the dog)

2. a) 600345
   ✎ *Hinweis: Z. 2*

   b) Marie won't be at work again until Friday.
   ✎ *Hinweis: "... she'll be back on Friday." (Z. 7)*

   c) 13th July to 21st July
   ✎ *Hinweis: Z. 16*

   d) a real breakfast
   ✎ *Hinweis: "I want breakfast – a real breakfast – not this continental bread roll that's called breakfast." (Z. 16/17)*

e) No, she probably doesn't smoke.
✎ *Hinweis: "Non-smoking, of course." (Z. 22)*
Sie sagt zwar nicht, dass sie nicht raucht, aber dass sie ein Nichtraucherzimmer reserviert, lässt darauf schließen, dass sie Nichtraucherin ist.

f) Humphrey is happier going by car
✎ *Hinweis: "Humphrey doesn't like planes or trains. He's much better travelling in a car." (Z. 25/26)*

g) he thinks she is taking a friend with her
✎ *Hinweis: "Oh, I see. You're travelling with someone else." (Z. 27)*
Der Ehemann kann nicht gemeint sein, da Frau Lawson bereits vorher im Gespräch deutlich macht, dass sie nicht verheiratet ist: "Actually, it's not Mrs Lawson, it's Ms Lawson." (Z. 13)

h) her pet
✎ *Hinweis: "Humphrey's my dog!" (Z. 46)*

3. ✎ *Hinweis: Bei diesen Fragen sollst du die Antworten nicht in ganzen Sätzen aufschreiben, sondern eine stimmige Antwort in ein bis fünf Wörtern geben. Das ist wichtig, denn in deiner Abschlussarbeit werden dir bei zu langen Antworten Punkte abgezogen.*

a) Who did Ms Lawson talk to the day before?	(she talked to) Marie
b) How will Ms Lawson get to Nice?	by car and ferry
c) Why does Ms Lawson need a single room with a lot of floor space?	for her (very large) dog
d) Has Ms Lawson been to the travel agent's before or has she only phoned them?	she has been there (before)

✎ *Hinweis*
zu a: "I think the name was ... Marie." (Z. 4/5)
zu b: "a ferry ticket just for me and the car" (Z. 32)
zu c: Humphrey darf nicht ins Bett, sondern muss auf dem Boden schlafen (Z. 31/32). Humphrey ist ein Irischer Wolfshund – eine sehr große Hunderasse (Z. 46/47).

zu d: Marie hat Humphrey einen Keks gegeben. Deswegen muss Ms Lawson schon einmal im Reisebüro gewesen sein. (Z. 47–51)

Listening Test 2: Waves on the water

Hinweis: Hier hörst du einen Dialog zwischen Liz und Tom, in dem Liz über ihre Erlebnisse in Schottland berichtet.

a) having a holiday
Hinweis: "What was Scotland like, Liz?" (Z. 1)

b) it often rains but there is usually some sunshine, too
Hinweis: "In the morning it rains, later the sun comes out and then it rains again." (Z. 2/3)

c) near water
Hinweis: "It's often misty as well, especially where there's water." (Z. 3/4)

d) Edinburgh
Hinweis: "We've been all over Scotland – Edinburgh, ..." (Z. 13)

e) a short time
Hinweis: "... for the last few days" (Z. 14/15)

f) from the USA
Hinweis: "full of American tourists" (Z. 27)

g) instruments
Hinweis: "bagpipes" (Z. 28)

h) in a peaceful place away from the main road
Hinweis: "... we were on the other side, the quiet side, camping." (Z. 28/29)

i) she was frightened
Hinweis: "Thought you said it was scary."/"It was. That's why I went to sleep." (Z. 35/36)

j) a large, dark object
Hinweis: "Something dark – big and dark in the water." (Z. 40)

k) a story to tease Tom
Hinweis: "I just wanted to see your face, when I said I'd seen the monster!" (Z. 48)

Listening Test 3: You need more than a flashy new moped

1. *Hinweis: Hier musst du den zehn Satzanfängen das richtige, d. h. das grammatikalisch und inhaltlich korrekte Satzende zuordnen. Da es mehr Enden als Satzanfänge gibt, musst du dir die Satzteile vor dem ersten Hören genau durchlesen. Höre beim ersten Anhören gut zu und beginne dann erst mit der Zuordnung.*

❶	❷	❸	❹	❺	❻	❼	❽	❾	❿
G	L	D	I	K	A	H	E	C	F

Hinweis
zu 1: "Are you doing anything?"/"Nothing much" (Z. 1/2)
zu 2: "Poor old Pete – spent all his money on his flashy new moped." (Z. 19)
zu 3: "Come on, tell big sis' what it's all about?" (Z. 19/20)
zu 4: "It's Jill Drake [...] I see her every day and just can't stop thinking about her." (Z. 23/24)
zu 5: "Tall, dark hair, thin, intelligent, happy, super-figure Jill Drake. You haven't got a chance." (Z. 25/26)
zu 6: "You're sweet – even for a brother – but not exactly romantic, you couldn't tell the difference between a rose and a potato." (Z. 33/34)
zu 7: "Come on, Susie – you're a girl – you've had thousands of boyfriends." (Z. 41/42)
zu 8: "Sell yourself, Pete. Just be you." (Z. 45/46)
zu 9: "Find something to go to – you know, a film or something, then just ask her if she'll come along." (Z. 46/47)
zu 10: "By the way, Pete, have you got Dave's number – you know, football Dave – year 11? (Z. 59/60)

2. a) she thinks he wants to talk about something.
   ✎ Hinweis: Diese Aufgabe kann am ehesten über das Ausschlussverfahren beantwortet werden. Susie liest einen Text für den Englischunterricht, als Pete sie anspricht, von Mathe ist keine Rede. Susies und Petes Mutter wird im Text ebenfalls mit keinem Wort erwähnt. Susie mag zwar ihren Bruder („You're sweet – even for a brother"), aber das ist nicht der Grund für ihr Interesse an dem Gespräch. Ihre Nachfragen am Gesprächsbeginn („And?" Z. 6 und 9) zeigen, dass sie vermutet, dass Pete mit ihr über etwas Bestimmtes sprechen möchte.

   b) he's embarrassed.
   ✎ Hinweis: "Oh man, that's so embarrassing. What if she says no? I'm left standing there – bright red, looking like a tomato feeling really stupid with everyone laughing at me ..." (Z. 48 – 50)

   c) hasn't got her number.
   ✎ Hinweis: "But I don't know her number, it's not in the book." (Z. 52)

   d) she wants to phone him.
   ✎ Hinweis: "Pete, have you got Dave's number – you know, football Dave – year 11?" (Z. 60)

Listening Test 4: Sightseeing in London

1. *✎ Hinweis: Unterstreiche die Sehenswürdigkeiten und Attraktionen, die die Mitarbeiterin des „London Eye" nennt.*

   a) <u>Big Ben and the Houses of Parliament</u>
   b) <u>Buckingham Palace</u>
   c) Shakespeare's Globe Theatre
   d) Tower of London
   e) <u>Madame Tussauds</u>
   f) <u>Westminster Abbey</u>
   g) Princess Diana Memorial Fountain
   h) <u>Trafalgar Square</u>
   i) <u>London Eye River Cruise</u>
   j) Tower Bridge

Hinweis: "… offering spectacular views of London and its famous landmarks, such as Big Ben and the Houses of Parliament, Buckingham Palace … Westminster Abbey and Trafalgar Square." (Z. 6–8); "Why not include a London Eye River Cruise in your experience?" (Z. 19); "You could follow up your flight with a visit to Madame Tussauds." (Z. 24)

2. *Hinweis: Bei diesen sieben Fragen sollst du knappe Antworten geben. Überschreite die Höchstzahl von sieben Wörtern nicht.*

a) What can you see on your London Eye ride?	the most important sights of London
b) How far can you see on a clear day?	25 miles
c) How long does a gradual ride take?	about 30 minutes
d) What is included in every ticket?	entry into 4 D Experience/entry into London Eye Entertainment centre
e) What can you enjoy in the entertainment centre? Name one thing.	unique views/a fantastic fireworks display/multi-sensory effects including wind, snow and bubbles
f) How can you avoid long queues?	buy a Fast Track Ticket (online)
g) What does the "horrible history" museum offer? Name one thing.	live actors/two scary rides/gruesome interactive effects

Hinweis
zu a: "… to see the most important sights of London" (Z. 3)
zu b: "On a clear day, you'll be able to have a 25 mile panoramic view." (Z. 4)
zu c: "The gradual flight […] takes approximately 30 minutes" (Z. 5/6)
zu d: "Included in every ticket is an entry into the 4 D Experience at the London Eye entertainment centre." (Z. 8–10)
zu e: "… unique views, a fantastic fireworks display and multi-sensory effects including wind, snow and bubbles" (Z. 11/12)
zu f: "If you buy this Fast Track Ticket online in advance, it is enough for you to arrive 15 minutes before you flight." (Z. 15–17)
zu g: "Life actors, two scary rides and gruesome interactive effects …" (Z. 29/30)

3. ✎ *Hinweis: Bei dieser Aufgabe musst du die Tabelle mit den Informationen aus dem Hörtext vervollständigen. Es sind keine ganzen Sätze gefordert, sondern lediglich einzelne Zahlen oder Stichwörter. Die Zahlen brauchst du nicht auszuschreiben.*

a) Number of capsules on the London Eye:	32
b) Three languages in which the audio tour on the river cruise is available:	French, German, Spanish, Dutch, Italian, Russian, Japanese, Mandarin Chinese
c) Maximum number of passengers in a private capsule:	25
d) The time the box office opens at the London Eye:	9.30 a.m.

✎ *Hinweis*
zu a: "32 high-tech glass capsules" (Z. 5)
zu b: Wenn du drei der Sprachen nennen kannst, die in den Zeilen 22/23 aufgezählt werden, ist das ausreichend.
zu c: "private capsule for 3 to 25 guests" (Z. 33/34)
zu d: "... you can ride the London Eye every day between 10.00 a.m. and 8.00 p.m. ... The ticket office opens half an hour before the first ride." (Z. 36–38)

Listening Test 5: Working abroad

✎ *Hinweis: Die Sprecher erzählen viel über sich selbst und ihre Erfahrungen im Ausland. Du musst also gut aufpassen, damit du alle Informationen zu Herkunftsland, bisheriger Aufenthaltsdauer, Ausbildung, Art der Arbeit und zum Gehalt verstehst, vor allem, weil die Informationen nicht immer in derselben Reihenfolge gegeben werden. Lies dir also zuerst einmal die Tabelle durch, damit du weißt, auf welche Details du im Hörtext achten musst. Während des ersten Hörens trägst du die Informationen, die du verstanden hast, in die Tabelle ein. Mache nach dem ersten Hördurchgang eine kurze Pause und überlege dir, auf welche Informationen du beim zweiten Durchgang besonders achten musst. Kontrolliere deine Antworten während des zweiten Hörens und ergänze die noch fehlenden Details.*

name	**country of origin**	**duration of stay so far**	**education**	**type of work**	**salary**
Tom	**Australia**	*not given*	**lifeguard**	**theme park**	£ 4.90/hour
Maria	**Brazil**	2 years	*not given*	**waitress**	*not given*
Heike	Belgium	**11 months**	**studies art**	**supermarket (clerk)**	*not given*
Rajiv	**India**	**one and a half years**	*not given*	*not given*	**minimum wage**
Jake	**South Africa**	**12 weeks**	law student	**au-pair**	**£ 230/ month**

Listening Test 6: Love and friendship

Hinweis: Hier nennen die Sprecher oft mehrere Details zu einem Tabellenfeld. Beschränke dich beim Ausfüllen der Tabelle jedoch auf die geforderte Anzahl an Informationen und notiere jeweils nur ein Detail pro Feld. Nur so schaffst du es, alle Felder zu bearbeiten. Lies dir außerdem vor dem ersten Hören die Tabelle genau durch – sollst du Informationen über den besten Freund/die beste Freundin und/oder über den Partner der Sprecher notieren?

	Bethany	**Shannon**	**Dave**	**Josh**	**Jake**
qualities of a best friend, boy- or girlfriend	honest/ funny	trust-worthy	*not given*	loyal/ trust-worthy/ upfront/ funny	upfront/ honest/ interesting/ good to talk to/ popular
things a best friend **should do**	tell her every-thing/ point out her faults/ make her laugh	keep secrets	respect him/ have time for him/ listen to him	have time to hang out	*not given*

	Bethany	Shannon	Dave	Josh	Jake
things a best friend **shouldn't do**	*not given*	*not given*	boast/ be arrogant/ talk about himself all the time/ not care for other people	*not given*	*not given*
outward **appearance of boy-/ girlfriend**	*not given*	*not given*	*not given*	*not given*	fit/good-looking/ well-dressed

Listening Test 7: Last weekend

1. ✎ *Hinweis: Hier hörst du, wie Sharon ihrer Freundin von ihrem letzten Wochenende erzählt. Beantworte die Fragen in höchstens sechs Wörtern.*

a) Who is Sharon talking to on the phone?	Laura
b) When was the party Sharon is talking about?	last weekend
c) What did she do at the beginning of the party?	she stood in the corner watching
d) What was the best thing about the boy she fancies?	his (dark brown) eyes/he was really entertaining/he told her hilarious stories
e) Why wasn't Sharon shy when she talked to the boy? Name one reason.	he was easy to talk to/ he really paid attention
f) What information does she have about the boy? Name three items.	Darren / 18/visiting a friend / he's from London
g) What interrupted their conversation?	a phone call
h) How did he excuse his leaving?	something urgent had come up
i) Why can't she contact him now?	she hasn't got his number/e-mail address

Hinweis
zu a: Z. 2
zu b: Z. 3/4
zu c: "At first I stood in the corner watching." (Z. 6/7)
zu d: Z. 13–16
zu e: Z. 18/19
zu f: Z. 15 und Z. 30/31
zu g: "... but then his phone rang." (Z. 20/21)
zu h: Z. 26/27
zu i: "... we didn't exchange phone numbers or e-mail addresses." (Z. 27/28)

2. *Hinweis: Versuche hier, nach dem Ausschlussverfahren vorzugehen und die falschen Antworten auszuschließen.*

   a) she fell in love with him immediately.
   Hinweis: "Right from the start I was totally head over heels and all." (Z. 11/12)

   b) her family and her hobbies.
   Hinweis: "... he seemed to want to know everything about me, about my family, my hobbies." (Z. 17/18)

   c) She asks Laura what to do.
   Hinweis: "What can I do, Laura?"(Z. 31)

Listening Test 8: My song

Hinweis: Bei dieser Aufgabe erzählen fünf Personen von einem Song, der sie an eine bestimmte Situation in ihrem Leben erinnert. Du musst jedem Sprecher den passenden Songtitel zuordnen.

❶	❷	❸	❹	❺
D	C	F	A	B

Hinweis
zu 1: "I was a student from Manchester [...] finding my way around Manhattan." (Z. 5–7)

zu 2: "... because it was on the corner you could always see your boyfriend coming ..." (Z. 15/16)
zu 3: "It isn't my country, is it? It's my wife's." (Z. 23)
zu 4: "My two friends and I were on summer camp in America." (Z. 26/27); "We were just kids having a wild time ..." (Z. 28/29)
zu 5: "... the song's not about wild animals at all" (Z. 32/33)

Listening Test 9: Something for everyone

✔ *Hinweis: Hier berichten fünf Jugendliche über ihre Festivalerfahrungen. Du musst die Aussagen den einzelnen Personen zuordnen. Eine Aussage bleibt übrig.*

Julie	Cassie	Laura	Mike	Lucy
E	**A**	**B**	**F**	**D**

✔ *Hinweis*
zu Julie: "... there were too many people drinking too much." (Z. 6)
zu Cassie: "... what got me were the loos" (Z. 10); "... someone should look after them – you pay enough to go." (Z. 13)
zu Laura: "... performances that are free and things happening in the street, which don't cost anything either" (Z. 17/18)
zu Mike: "... my parents took me to a country show" (Z. 22)
zu Lucy: "Anyone can take part ..." (Z. 30)
Die Antwortmöglichkeit C bleibt übrig.

Listening Test 10: Chill out with Chill

✔ *Hinweis: Für diese zehn Fragen gibt es wieder jeweils vier Antwortmöglichkeiten. Versuche, die falschen Antworten auszuschließen.*

a) New York
✔ *Hinweis: "a New York rapper" (Z. 2)*

b) concerts
✔ *Hinweis: "... currently touring New England with his band." (Z. 2/3)*

c) blacks in the southern states of America
Hinweis: "Sure – in other black music – the gospel singers in the South" (Z. 7)

d) because there are many social problems there
Hinweis: "... tough lives, there's no work, no money, and gangs" (Z. 12/13)

e) relationships, politics and inner-city life
Hinweis: "Rappers use relationships, political issues ... and life in inner-city America ..." (Z. 16/17)

f) because they are involved in the violence
Hinweis: "They're often in the middle of these problems, too." (Z. 21/22)

g) African-American disc jockeys
Hinweis: "Rap started in private parties with black DJs making their own sounds ..." (Z. 24)

h) new sounds and stories
Hinweis: "... making their own sounds" (Z. 24); "... making a new sound" (Z. 28); "... to tell stories above their new sounds" (Z. 31)

i) The largest demand for rap music comes from young white people.
Hinweis: "Seventy-five percent of rap music is bought by white kids." (Z. 34/35) Hier musst du wissen, dass „demand" Nachfrage heißt.

j) everyone hears about their lives
Hinweis: "... the stories of African-Americans are being heard." (Z. 35)

▶ Lösungen zum Kompetenzbereich Leseverstehen

Allgemeiner Hinweis: In diesem Kapitel wird dein Leseverständnis überprüft. Da du hier die Möglichkeit hast, den Text mehrmals durchzulesen, werden manchmal genauere Details abgefragt als in den Aufgaben zum Hörverstehen. Lies dir den Lesetext zunächst durch und markiere dir Wörter, die du gar nicht verstehst, die aber für das Verständnis unbedingt nötig sind, mit Textmarker und schlage sie nach dem ersten Lesen nach. Lies dir nun die Aufgabenstellung und die Aufgaben genau durch und nimm dir den Lesetext ein zweites Mal vor. Markiere dabei die Textstellen, die für die Lösung der Aufgaben jeweils ausschlaggebend sind, mit einem andersfarbigen Textmarker und trage die Lösungen ein. Überprüfe deine Antworten in einem weiteren Durchgang noch einmal und vergleiche sie anschließend mit den Lösungen im Lösungsband. Wenn du eine falsche Antwort gegeben hast, solltest du dir überlegen, warum deine Antwort falsch war. Vergleiche deine markierte Textstelle mit der Angabe der Textstelle im Hinweis zur Lösung. Stimmen sie überein? Hast du den Textabschnitt richtig verstanden? Schlage noch weitere Wörter im Wörterbuch nach, wenn du dir unsicher bist. Hast du die Aufgabe oder Frage genau gelesen? Lies noch einmal nach. Wenn du verstanden hast, wieso deine Lösung falsch war, wird dir so ein Fehler sicherlich beim nächsten Mal nicht mehr passieren und du wirst immer besser im Umgang mit Lesetexten.

Reading Test 1: A holiday on the water

Hinweis: In dieser Aufgabe musst du mithilfe des Textes entscheiden, ob die Aussagen richtig oder falsch sind. Anschließend sollst du die richtige Textstelle angeben, an der du die relevante Information gefunden hast. Lies die Aufgabenstellung immer ganz genau, damit du weißt, was von dir verlangt wird.
Bereits beim ersten Blick auf diesen Lesetext erkennst du an der Anrede und Verabschiedung, dass es sich um einen Brief handelt. Mit dem Pronomen „I" ist im Text daher immer Sam gemeint.

1. a) **true**
   justification: **I've just had** ...
   Hinweis: "I've just had a really great holiday with my parents." (Z. 2)

   b) **false**
   justification: **In England there are** ...
   Hinweis: Für die richtige Lösung ist das Verb „hire" („mieten") ein wichtiges Schlüsselwort, denn Sam schreibt: "In England there are many different types of boat that you can hire." (Z. 5/6)

   c) **false**
   justification: **A week on a** .../ **It was a lot** ...
   Hinweis: "A week on a boat sounds boring but it wasn't. It was a lot of fun." (Z. 17/18)

   d) **true**
   justification: **You are not allowed** ...
   Hinweis: "You are not allowed to sail at night so you have to stop when it is getting dark." (Z. 27/28)

   e) **true**
   justification: **But I discovered the** ...
   Hinweis: "But I discovered the countryside isn't very quiet." (Z. 30/31)

   f) **false**
   justification: **Why I'm telling** ...
   Hinweis: "Why I'm telling you all this is that I'd love to go again but my parents don't want to." (Z. 34/35)

   g) **true**
   justification: **I can send you** ...
   Hinweis: "I can send you some pictures if you want." (Z. 40)

2. a) the holiday was going to be different.
   Hinweis: "Normally I don't go on holiday with them but they decided that they wanted a different type of holiday this year." (Z. 2–4)

   b) somewhere different.
   Hinweis: Z. 18–22

c) were made by people.
Hinweis: Für die richtige Beantwortung dieser Aufgabe musst du das Schlüsselwort „monks" („Mönche") verstehen, denn die Norfolk Broads „were made by monks a long time ago". (Z. 24)

d) there weren't any streetlights.
Hinweis: "... there are no streetlights" (Z. 30)

e) aren't interested in another holiday on the water.
Hinweis: "... but my parents don't want to." (Z. 34/35)

f) are interested in a holiday together on the Broads.
Hinweis: "Would you like to come with me in the summer holidays?" (Z. 35); "Let me know if you are interested." (Z. 37/38)

g) more than £ 300.
Hinweis: Z. 36/37 (about £ 300 + travel from Germany)

h) it will help you.
Hinweis: "... it's good for your English" (Z. 38/39)

Reading Test 2: Earning, working, learning

Hinweis: In dieser Aufgabe musst du mithilfe des Textes entscheiden, ob die Aussagen richtig oder falsch sind. Anschließend sollst du die richtige Textstelle angeben, an der du die relevante Information gefunden hast. Beachte, dass du hier die ersten vier Wörter des entsprechenden Satzes angeben sollst.

1. a) **false**
justification: **These jobs used to** .../**Many of these young** ...
Hinweis: Ein wichtiger Ausdruck zum richtigen Verständnis ist hier „used to be" („waren früher/waren gewöhnlich"), denn daraus folgt, dass es eine Veränderung gegeben hat: "These jobs used to be mainly weekend or holiday ones but today the situation is changing." (Z. 2–4); "Many of these young people now work up to fifteen hours a week and not just at weekends or in their holidays." (Z. 8–11)

b) **true**
justification: **The main areas of** …
Hinweis: Die Lösung findest du in den Zeilen 12 –14. Das Wort „retail" bedeutet „Einzelhandel", ist aber für die Beantwortung der Frage nicht unbedingt nötig, da im Text die gleichen Beispiele wie in der Aufgabenstellung folgen: "The main areas of work are in the retail industry, for example in shops and in supermarkets"

c) **false**
justification: **Traditional part-time workers are** …
Hinweis: "Traditional part-time workers are often women with children who do not want to work … at the weekends." (Z. 18–22)

d) **true**
justification: **In a perfect world** …
Hinweis: "In a perfect world it might be best to learn first and work later but many young people … need to earn money." (Z. 32–35)

e) **true**
justification: **They learn to work** …
Hinweis: "They learn to work with other people and often have responsibilities for the first time in their lives." (Z. 42–45)

f) **true**
justification: **Many students often add** …
Hinweis: "Many students … learn to understand other people better." (Z. 53–56)

g) **false**
justification: **Schools, of course, do** …
Hinweis: "Schools, of course, do not support the idea of earning and learning." (Z. 67/68)

h) **false**
justification: **They complain of students** …
Hinweis: "They complain of students … missing lessons." (Z. 68–73)

i) **true**
justification: **Almost 40 % of 15–24-year-olds** …
Hinweis: "Almost 40 % of 15 – 24-year-olds have had no health or safety training by their employers." (Z. 89–91)

2.

❶	❷	❸	❹	❺	❻
C	E	A	F	G	D

✒ *Hinweis*
zu 1: Hier musst du nun wissen oder aus dem Kontext erschließen, dass „retail“ „Einzelhandel“ bedeutet. Die Lösung steht im Text in den Zeilen 12–14.
zu 2: “Employers need workers for these unattractive times to work. This means, therefore, that there are a lot of jobs for young people which fit nicely around a school day.” (Z. 22–26)
zu 3: “... many young people find that they need to earn money.” (Z. 33–35)
zu 4: “If they do not do their job properly, for example, they can easily lose it.” (Z. 47–49)
zu 5: Z. 58–66
Hier würde auch Antwortmöglichkeit D passen. Allerdings bleibt dann für Nummer Sechs keine passende Lösung mehr übrig.
zu 6: “... they must also understand that there are dangers in the world of work.” (Z. 85–87)
Die Antwortmöglichkeit B bleibt übrig.

Reading Test 3: The hunters and the hunted: who’s for dinner?

1. ✒ *Hinweis: Bei dieser Aufgabe sollst du den Textabschnitten jeweils eine Überschrift zuordnen. Zwei Überschriften bleiben dabei übrig.*

A	B	C	D	E	F	G	H
❻	❺	❶	❾	❽	❸	❿	❹

✒ *Hinweis: Die Überschriften „Hopping, skipping and jumping“ und „The Europeans“ bleiben übrig.*

2. a) been the same for a very long time.
✒ *Hinweis: Z. 6–9*

b) how to behave in crocodile areas.
✒ *Hinweis: Z. 24–26*

c) can live on one meal for a long time.
Hinweis: Z. 34/35

d) stay away from the edge of the water as far as possible.
Hinweis: Z. 42–46

e) must leave it alone because it is protected.
Hinweis: Z. 51–53

f) live in trees.
Hinweis: Z. 58/59

g) hop at 60 kmh and jump three metres high.
Hinweis: Z. 61–63

h) for food and for their skins.
Hinweis: Z. 67–69

i) more kangaroos than people.
Hinweis: Z. 77–79

3.

❶	❷	❸	❹	❺	❻
F	D	B	E	G	A

Hinweis
zu 1: "These crocodiles have no enemies and can live to a very old age; some are thought to be over 100 years old." (Z. 20–23)
zu 2: "Although it is called a saltwater crocodile, it lives happily in rivers …" (Z. 18–20)
zu 3: "Firstly, you should stay out of the water …" (Z. 39/40)
zu 4: Die Textstellen „… another protected species is the kangaroo" (Z. 54/55) und „Four types of kangaroos are still hunted …" (Z. 70/71) werden für die richtige Zuordnung benötigt.
zu 5: "They also like to live in groups …" (Z. 63)
zu 6: "… the kangaroos are not kept on farms." (Z. 82/83)
Die Antwortmöglichkeit C bleibt übrig.

4. ✎ *Hinweis: Hier musst du die Antworten zu den Fragen im Text finden. Es hilft dir, wenn du die Antworten im Text unterstreichst. Denk daran, dass du nur 1–7 Wörter schreiben sollst. Schreibe also nur Stichwörter und keine ganzen Sätze auf.*

a) What is Australia famous for?	(for its) colourful wildlife
b) Who brought horses to Australia?	the Europeans/early settlers
c) What did the flu cause to many Native Australians?	many Aboriginal people/Natives died/ it killed them
d) What do Australians have to be careful about? Name one thing.	saltwater crocodiles/sharks/scorpions/ mosquitoes/snakes
e) Why do you need nets at night?	you can be bitten by mosquitoes/there are mosquitoes which carry diseases
f) Why don't people have to be too afraid of snakes?	they only attack if they feel threatened/ they normally don't attack

Reading Test 4: An interview

1. ✎ *Hinweis: In dieser Aufgabe musst du mithilfe des Textes entscheiden, ob die Aussagen richtig oder falsch sind. Anschließend sollst du die richtige Textstelle angeben, an der du die relevante Information gefunden hast. Hierbei kannst du entweder den Satzanfang (die ersten vier Wörter) eintragen, wie in der folgenden Lösung oder die relevante Stelle innerhalb des Satzes. Manchmal sind hier mehrere Stellen richtig, von denen du aber nur eine angeben musst.*

   a) **true**
   justification: **My name is John** …
   ✎ *Hinweis: "My name is John Lumsden, I'm 26 and I come from Dublin in Ireland." (Z. 2–4)*

   b) **false**
   justification: **We met in Ireland** …
   ✎ *Hinweis: Der Hauptgrund war seine Freundin: "We met in Ireland and lived there together for quite a long time but she didn't really like it, so we decided to move to Munich." (Z. 7–10)*

c) **true**
justification: **She didn't like the** … / **If it's not actually** …
Hinweis: "She didn't like the weather in Ireland either, because it was always cloudy or raining." (Z. 17–19); "If it's not actually raining, then it's going to rain soon." (Z. 21/22)

d) **false**
justification: **I should try more** …
Hinweis: "I should try more but everyone here speaks such fantastic English." (Z. 48–50)

e) **true**
justification: **I think German kids** …
Hinweis: "I think German kids have it much harder. They have to learn English." (Z. 58–60)

f) **false**
justification: **When I visit home** …
Hinweis: "When I visit home, I always come back with lots of tea bags, Irish sausages and other things in my suitcase." (Z. 78–81)

g) **true**
justification: **I've learnt to** … / **I've even started** …
Hinweis: "I've learnt to ski here and it's great fun." (Z. 84/85); "I've even started going walking in the Alps." (Z. 92/93)

2. *Hinweis: Bei dieser Aufgabe musst du Fragen zum Text beantworten. Es hilft dir, wenn du die relevanten Textstellen unterstreichst. Denk daran, dass du nur bis zu sechs Wörter schreiben sollst. Schreibe also keine ganzen Sätze auf. Manchmal sind auch mehrere Antworten möglich, aber du brauchst nur eine zu geben, außer wenn zwei gefordert sind („Name two …").*

a) Where is John's workplace?	just outside Munich
b) What does John's girlfriend think about Dublin?	it's too big and grey / she doesn't like it
c) Why can it be difficult to understand Irish people living in the country?	they speak fast and not clearly / they have strong accents

d) Why can't John go skiing in Ireland? (name two reasons)	it doesn't snow very often
	there aren't any ski slopes
e) What did John do in his free time in Dublin?	he watched football on TV

✎ Hinweis
zu a: Z. 4
zu b: Z. 16/17
zu c: Z. 35–39
zu d: Z. 86–89
zu e: Z. 93/94

3. *✎ Hinweis: Für diese Aufgabe musst du die Textabschnitte den vorgegebenen Überschriften zuordnen. Eine Überschrift passt allerdings zu keinem der Textabschnitte.*

Leisure time	G	The school system	–
Language learning	E	Talking to Germans	D
Language and accents	C	John's background	A
Reasons for moving	B	The tastes of Ireland	F

Reading Test 5: Charities

1. *✎ Hinweis: Bei dieser Aufgabe gehst du am besten schrittweise vor. Lies dir den ersten Text durch und suche dann den passenden Satz bzw. das passende Satzende dazu aus. Nur einer der vier angebotenen Sätze ist richtig. Du musst genau lesen. Gehe bei den anderen drei Texten ebenso vor.*

   a) supports families and children who haven't got a lot of money.
   ✎ Hinweis: "Action now helps very poor families and their children ..."/ "We help these poor families ..."

   b) They rescue people and animals.
   ✎ Hinweis: "... sometimes we rescue people who have fallen down a cliff"; "... sometimes we even have to rescue someone's pet"

c) takes care of injured birds and animals.
Hinweis: "We even have our own hospitals for injured animals and birds …"

d) restores old houses.
Hinweis: "We like to rebuild them and make them beautiful again."

2.

❶	❷	❸	❹	❺
G	F	A	B	E

Hinweis
zu 1: "ActionNow helps very poor families …"; "Our members risk their lives every day saving other people." (RNLI)
zu 2: "Most people are volunteers." (RNLI)
zu 3: "… and keep it as a place of special interest for people to enjoy."(Wild Trust); "… then you're supporting your heritage for future generations to enjoy". (Don't Fall Down)
zu 4: "It starts village schools so children can learn to read, write and do Maths."
zu 5: "The Royal National Lifeboat Institution is an emergency service for the sea."
Die Antwortmöglichkeiten C und D bleiben übrig.

Reading Test 6: The Royal Theatre

In dieser Aufgabe musst du die Antworten zu den Fragen in den drei Annoncen finden. Es hilft dir, wenn du die Lösungen im Text unterstreichst. Denk daran, dass du nur 1–5 Wörter oder Zahlen schreiben sollst.

a) Who wrote *Robinson Crusoe?*	Daniel Defoe
b) When do the afternoon performances of *Robinson Crusoe* start?	(at) 2.30 p.m.
c) How much does it cost for two children (7 and 13) to go to *Robinson Crusoe?*	£ 7

d) What day can't you go to see *Summer Holiday?*	Friday
e) Who is Bobby?	she is a famous singer/a famous singer in disguise
f) Who do the witches talk to?	Macbeth
g) How long does Macbeth take?	150 minutes

Reading Test 7: Adam would like to have a girlfriend, but he can't

1. ✎ *Hinweis: Dir werden sieben Satzanfänge vorgegeben. Deine Aufgabe ist es, den Anfängen die richtigen, d. h. die grammatikalisch und inhaltlich korrekten Satzenden zuzuordnen.*

❶	❷	❸	❹	❺	❻	❼
K	G	J	F	H	I	A

✎ *Hinweis*
zu 1: "Because I knew she'd leave me. Like everyone else."(Z. 6/7); "It would be great if she was my girlfriend but just the idea of losing her freaks me out." (Z. 77–79)
zu 2: "Before Dad died when I was fourteen, I was like any other teenage boy – playing football and computer games with my mates." (Z. 8–11)
zu 3: "Dad loved kidding around with us, while my mum was the one we went to with our problems." (Z. 13–15)
zu 4: "He'd had a heart attack, and the paramedics couldn't help him come back ..." (Z. 21–23)
zu 5: "I believe it's her way of dealing with the situation – at work she doesn't have the time to think about what happened ..." (Z. 29–32)
zu 6: "I stopped meeting my friends in the afternoons and going out as it felt safer at home ..." (Z. 48 – 52)
zu 7: "Losing my dad and – in a way – my mum, too ..." (Z. 62/63)
Die Antwortmöglichkeiten B, C, D und E bleiben übrig.

2. *Hinweis: Hier musst du ankreuzen, ob die Aussagen zum Text richtig oder falsch sind. Außerdem hast du vier Wörter des Satzes anzugeben, in dem du die Information für deine Antwort gefunden hast. Manchmal kommen hier mehrere Sätze in Frage. Wähle den Satz aus, der die wichtigsten Informationen enthält. In dieser Lösung sind die ersten vier Wörter des entsprechenden Satzes angegeben.*

   a) **false**
   justification: **It wasn't that** …
   Hinweis: Adams Freund flirtet mit Ruth und Adam ist in Eliza verliebt: "It wasn't that I didn't like Eliza – I really did …" (Z. 4/5)

   b) **true**
   justification: **The thing is though** …
   Hinweis: Von Zeile 26–37 wird der Zustand der Mutter beschrieben, aber die entscheidende Information kommt erst gegen Ende dieses Abschnitts: "The thing is though, Sophie and I don't see her at all anymore" (Z. 34–36)

   c) **false**
   justification: **I really like her** …
   Hinweis: Adam sind andere Paare egal: "'… I really like her', I just shrugged, because I couldn't imagine caring about someone that way anymore." (Z. 59–62)

   d) **false**
   justification: **I've got plans** …
   Hinweis: Um diese Frage richtig zu beantworten, musst du wissen, dass ein „paramedic" ein Sanitäter ist: "I've got plans for the future: I want to train as a paramedic …" (Z. 69/70)

   e) **true**
   justification: **She's one of** …
   Hinweis: "She's one of the most popular girls in my year … and I couldn't believe my luck, when I found out that she fancied me." (Z. 73–77)

   f) **false**
   justification: **I really want to** …

Hinweis: Adam sagt nicht, dass er es sich nie wieder vorstellen kann, jemanden zu lieben, sondern er sagt, dass er sich selbst erst über einiges klar werden muss, bevor er eine Beziehung eingehen kann: "I really want to be with someone eventually, but I have to sort my head out before I can even think about having a relationship." (Z. 87–90)

Reading Test 8: The Australian Aboriginal people

1. *Hinweis: Schreibe hier nicht einfach den Satz aus dem Text ab, sondern beschränke dich auf ein bis acht Wörter. Bei einigen Fragen musst du nur einen von mehreren im Text vorkommenden Aspekten nennen.*

a) How long have Aboriginal people been living in Australia?	for at least 40,000 years
b) How did Aboriginal people live together?	in family groups
c) What is one of the most important things for Aboriginal people?	(their) land
d) Who would be gatherers?	women and children
e) Why was it important that the Aboriginal people understood nature well?	they needed to know how to get food
f) What describes Elders the best?	clever older Aboriginal people with particular skills
g) Why did many Aboriginal people die when the Europeans arrived?	the Europeans killed many / the Europeans brought diseases with them
h) What happened to many children with white fathers and Aboriginal mothers? Name one aspect.	they were taken away from their families/ they were brought up in white families
i) Why is the Australian government trying to help the Aboriginal people? Name one reason.	because Aboriginal people were badly discriminated against / because they have many problems / because many of them can't find jobs / because they often have poor lives / because many Aboriginal people have lost their culture

Hinweis:
zu a: "… for at least 40,000 years" (Z. 4/5)
zu b: "They usually lived in family groups" (Z. 9/10)
zu c: "Land is very important for the Aboriginal people." (Z. 13/14)
zu d: "… women and children did the gathering." (Z. 31/32)
zu e: "They had to know when and where they could get something to eat …" (Z. 35/36)
zu f: Z. 40–49
zu g: "… they were shot and killed" (Z. 58); "Also, the Europeans brought illnesses that had not existed in Australia before, for example influenza, which killed many more." (Z. 60–65)
zu h: "… children were taken away from their Aboriginal families. These children were then given to white people …" (Z. 69–73)
zu i: Z. 81–89

2. *Hinweis: Bei dieser Aufgabe sind sechs Satzanfänge vorgegeben und du musst das passende Ende finden. Jedes Ende darf nur einmal benutzt werden.*

❶	❷	❸	❹	❺	❻
D	H	E	B	A	G

Hinweis:
zu 1: "Until European settlers arrived in Australia, the Aboriginal people people were able to cherish their traditional culture without much outside influence." (Z. 5–9)
zu 2: "… Uluru, which the European colonisers called Ayers Rock" (Z. 17–19)
zu 3: "All adult Aboriginal men were equal" (Z. 40)
zu 4: "Aboriginal people were not farmers …" (Z. 28/29); "The Europeans wanted the land for themselves to start new lives, usually as farmers." (Z. 55–57)
zu 5: Z. 50–55
zu 6: Z. 81–85
Die Antwortmöglichkeiten C und F bleiben übrig.

Reading Test 9: I was bullied on Facebook

1. ✎ *Hinweis: Hier werden dir zehn Satzanfänge vorgegeben. Deine Aufgabe ist es, den Anfängen die richtigen, d. h. die grammatikalisch und inhaltlich korrekten Satzenden zuzuordnen. Da es mehr Endungen als Anfänge gibt, musst du sehr genau lesen.*

   a) enjoyed what she was doing.
   ✎ *Hinweis: "… she was proud of it." (Z. 19/20)*

   b) but didn't take any drastic action.
   ✎ *Hinweis: "Although the school intervened immediately, it decided not to exclude the bully …" (Z. 30–32)*

   c) helped her go back to school.
   ✎ *Hinweis: "… friends persuaded her to do it. Christine's friends have rallied around her, trying to make things easier for her at school …" (Z. 37–40)*

   d) tried to get Christine to think about something else.
   ✎ *Hinweis: "… so they tried to talk about other things to distract me." (Z. 45/46)*

   e) she is trying to forget what has happened to her.
   ✎ *Hinweis: "I've tried to push what happened to me to the back of my mind …" (Z. 49–51)*

   f) people know what she had done.
   ✎ *Hinweis: "I thought she was probably just sorry that she'd got found out." (Z. 57–59)*

   g) they may change the rules about bullying.
   ✎ *Hinweis: "… the school 'would look at revising the cyber-bullying policy'" (Z. 63/64)*

   h) she is taking her final exams soon.
   ✎ *Hinweis: "… we start our GCSEs soon" (Z. 67)*

   i) life can become very difficult for the person who has been bullied.
   ✎ *Hinweis: Hier musst du den gesamten Text einbeziehen. Der Text beschreibt die Situation eines Mobbingopfers detailliert, deshalb musst du dich für diese Antwort entscheiden.*

Reading Test 10: Tennis – a game with a long history

❶	❷	❸	❹	❺	❻	❼	❽	❾	❿
C	H	B	J	I	E	A	M	L	F

Hinweis

zu 1: "Tennis is a game that has been played for a very long time ..." (Z. 1/2)

zu 2: "The most common view ... is that French monks were the first to play the game in their courtyards ..." (Z. 9–12)

zu 3: "By 1500 ... the wooden ball had been replaced by a more suitable leather ball." (Z. 28–31)

zu 4: "In France, even the Royal Family played the game [...] Henry VII and Henry VIII [...] are known to have loved playing it." (Z. 34–38)

zu 5: "At Hampton Court, a player gained the most points when he managed to hit a wooden portrait of Henry VIII." (Z. 55–58)

zu 6: "The popularity of tennis ... increased again when a bouncier tennis ball made out of rubber was invented. From then on tennis could be played outside on grass, too." (Z. 58–64)

zu 7: "He designed the court, which was shorter than the modern one, to look like an hourglass with its tightest part at the net." (Z. 68–71)

zu 8: "In 1877, the All England Club Croquet held the first professional tennis championships in Wimbledon ..." (Z. 78–80)

zu 9: "It is the aim of every professional tennis player to win all four 'Grand Slam' championships within a year." (Z. 92–95)

zu 10: "If you want to be fit, grab a racket and head out for an invigorating game of tennis." (Z. 100–102)

Die Antwortmöglichkeiten D, G und K bleiben übrig.

Reading Test 11: Signs

Hinweis: Bei dieser Aufgabe werden dir Schilder vorgelegt. Deine Aufgabe ist es, zu entscheiden, welche der vier Aussagen auf das jeweilige Schild zutrifft. Bist du dir einmal unsicher, welche Aussage die richtige ist, kannst du versuchen, die Antwort durch Ausschluss der falschen Lösungen zu erschließen.

1. Your $ 7 will be returned on the day of departure if your room is tidy.
   Hinweis: "A $ 7 deposit is required and will be returned at the end of your stay."; "On departure day, you are responsible for cleaning your own room. Your deposit will be returned upon room inspection."

2. If you want a shop assistant to bring you a different size, you can call him/her by pressing a button.
   Hinweis: "If you need assistance, feel free to press the call button next to the mirror. A shop assistant will come as soon as possible."
   Aussage A ist falsch, da es heißt: "Return all items you do not intend to buy to the shop assistant." B ist inkorrekt, da auf dem Schild steht: "No chewing gum, food or drink allowed in the changing rooms." Auch C trifft nicht auf den Text zu: "Only 5 items permitted in the changing room at one time."

3. Nude sunbathing is not permitted for teenagers and adults.
   Hinweis: "Bathing suits must be worn at all times. Children under 2 are exempt from this rule."

4. She feels comfortable in the zoo.
   Hinweis: "She has adjusted well to the zoo …"

▶ Lösungen zum Kompetenzbereich Schreiben

Allgemeiner Hinweis: Lies dir die Arbeitsschritte zum Verfassen eines Textes im Kapitel Schreiben genau durch. Wenn du nach diesen Schritten vorgehst, wird es dir nicht mehr schwerfallen, einen guten Text zu schreiben. Die Lösungen zu den Schreibaufgaben sind Vorschläge. Lass dich nicht davon entmutigen, wenn deine Lösung von der Musterlösung abweicht. Die Vorschläge können dir als Anhaltspunkt dienen, wie die Lösung aussehen kann. Vergleiche deine Lösung inhaltlich mit der Beispiellösung und überarbeite sie anschließend sprachlich, indem du Wendungen aus der Beispiellösung in deinen Text einbaust.

1. *Hinweis: Hier werden dir Stichpunkte, die dir das inhaltliche Gerüst für den Brief liefern, vorgegeben. Denke an das Layout eines Briefes. Vergiss nicht, dass du einen Brief an einen Freund schreibst. Das sollte aus den Wendungen, die du benutzt, hervorgehen.*

(address)
(date)

(your friend's name and address)
Dear Sam,
Hello, how are you? I'm fine. I'm on a school trip to Cambridge, and yesterday we saw a group of musicians playing in the street outside a shop. They played really good music. It was some kind of Gipsy music and it was a great act. They even got a young boy from the crowd to play with them. That was very funny. The people around us were dancing and clapping in time with the music, and we all enjoyed ourselves. And guess what – even Mr Hill, our teacher, was dancing! That was the funniest thing I have ever seen. They were also selling their CDs for £ 10. I really wanted to buy one, but I didn't have enough money. Luckily one of my classmates bought one, so I can probably borrow it from him. We listened to the group for a long time and we put a few pounds in the hat they passed round. I'll show you the pics I've taken when we see each other again. I hope to see you soon.
Best wishes,
Noah *(181 words)*

2. ✎ *Hinweis: Bei diesem Brief ist es wichtig, dass du alle Fragen aufführst, damit du auch alle benötigten Informationen erhältst. Natürlich sollte der Brief besonders höflich verfasst sein, denn du möchtest Auskünfte über das Angebot haben und du kennst die Person nicht, der du diesen Brief schreibst.*

(address)
(date)

Mike Johnson
BritHols
36 Luton Road
Bedford
BD9 RT5

Dear Mr Johnson,
My name is Leonie Meyer and I am from the north of Germany. I saw your advert in *The Daily News* for a holiday in Britain. I would like to visit London because I never been there before and I have read a lot about this interesting city. I would therefore like to ask you for some more information. Could you tell me whereabouts in London the hotel is? I would like to visit London for one week in August 10th –17th and I would like a single room. Are the rooms en-suite? Does the hotel have a restaurant where I could have an evening meal? Does it offer vegetarian dishes?
I am very interested in the sights and old buildings, so I would also like to go on a city tour. Could you send me some information about them too, including the price?
I'm looking forward to hearing from you.
Yours sincerely,
Leonie Meyer *(168 words)*

3. ✎ *Hinweis: Hier bewirbst du dich per E-Mail um einen Job und solltest höfliche Formulierungen verwenden, damit du den Empfänger auch davon überzeugen kannst, dass du die oder der Richtige für diese Tätigkeit bist.*

An: LucyMacdonald@Farmlands.co.uk
Betreff: work experience at Farmlands

Dear Ms Macdonald,
I am interested in a work experience placement at Farmlands and would be grateful for some more information. My name is Julia Mertens and I live in Germany. I am 16 years old and have just completed my school-

leaving exams. I hope to work in the tourism industry and would like to improve my English and gain work experience before I start looking for an apprenticeship.
Please could you tell me whereabouts in Scotland Farmlands is and what I would be doing there? In your advert you write that accommodation and meals are available, but would I have to pay for these? If so, how much would they cost? Could you please also tell me how long I would have to work each day and on which days I would have to work? I would also like to know how much I would be paid. I would be happy to discuss all this with you over the phone.
I am looking forward to hearing from you.
Yours sincerely,
Julia Mertens *(178 words)*

4. *Hinweis: In dieser Aufgabe schreibst du eine E-Mail an einen Freund/eine Freundin, der/die nach Europa reisen will. Denk daran, die E-Mail-Adresse und einen Betreff zu ergänzen. Du beschreibst in deiner E-Mail deinen letzten Besuch in London und versuchst deinen Freund/deine Freundin davon zu überzeugen, dass London eine äußerst sehenswerte Stadt ist.*

An: G.blue@yahoo.au
Betreff: my stay in London

Hi Garry,
Gosh, I've just had a wonderful time in London. We only got back a couple of days ago. My friend Louisa and I went there for a long weekend. People always say London is so expensive and that travelling is expensive too, but here in Kiel we have a travel agent who offers cheap short trips to European capitals. We only paid € 99 per person for the bus trip there and the hostel in the city centre. Anyway, London is a fascinating place. You really have to go there when you come to Europe. We only had a couple of days for sightseeing, but we wanted to see as much as possible and do some serious shopping. We started by looking at the government buildings in Westminster, including the Houses of Parliament with Big Ben. We also saw Buckingham Palace. Unfortunately the Queen wasn't in. The Tower of London is an absolute must, so is Madame Tussauds.
You really mustn't miss London when you come over.
Take care! Jenny *(177 words)*

5. ✐ *Hinweis: In dieser Aufgabe geht es darum, einen Blogeintrag zu verfassen, in dem du deinen Lesern deine Situation zu Hause mit deinen Eltern beschreibst. Berichte darüber, ob du Schwierigkeiten mit dem Schulstoff hast. Frage deine Leser*innen, was sie von der Einstellung deiner Eltern halten und ob sie dir einen Rat geben können. Am Ende solltest du sagen, wie du mit der Situation umgehen wirst.*

   Hey folks,
   Here's the latest news on the "parents' front". As I wrote in my entry last week, I'll be taking my final exams in two months, and now my parents are running wild. They don't want me to see my boyfriend anymore until after the exams. They think this isn't the right time to be going out with friends and they want me to study all the time. That's unbelievable. I mean two months is such a long time to go, and I think I'm already quite prepared. Besides, my marks are not that bad, and I'm not the first person to take the GCSE, am I? Are all parents like mine?
   My boyfriend is really good at school and he always helps me with my homework, so I simply have to see him on a regular basis if I want good marks.
   What do you think about my parents' decision? Do you have the same problems? I think I'm going to ask my boyfriend's parents if they could talk to my parents. They are really nice and understanding and they'd probably support my boyfriend and me.
   Looking forward to your stories and your advice.
   CU ☺ Maria-Lina *(198 words)*

6. ✐ *Hinweis: In dieser Aufgabe sollst du einen Artikel für eine Schülerzeitung verfassen, in dem du über die Ansichten zweier indischer Freunde zum Thema „arrangierte Ehen" schreibst. Da auch nach deiner Meinung gefragt wird, solltest du dir überlegen, wie du zu dem Thema stehst. Baue deine Argumentation geschickt auf und erwähne auch die Gegenargumente. Deine Argumentation muss schlüssig und geordnet sein.*

   Arranged Marriages – a Chance for Love?
   by Sandy Müller
   Many people from the Western world are against arranged marriages. I have talked to two friends from India about the subject and this is what they think about it:

Pria (16) belives that a couple should only marry if they are madly in love, and that a marriage between two people who were chosen by their parents cannot be happy: both will have to enter into the marriage without really knowing what their future partner will be like. If you choose your partner, you are familiar with his or her faults and so, if you finally decide to get married, you know what to expect. But of course, there is never any guarantee that you will always be happy together.
Raschesch (16) has a different opinion about the subject. He lives in a very traditional family, and the marriages of his parents and uncles and aunts were all arranged, but everyone still lives together happily. Meanwhile, 80 per cent of his classmates' parents are divorced and have married new partners. His classmates suffer from this situation.
To sum up, I think that, although an arranged marriage and a love match start off differently, there is the chance of a "happily ever after" in both cases.
Personally, however, I would not want my parents to choose a partner for me. I want to fall in love and decide for myself whether I want to spend the rest of my life with that person. *(251 words)*

7. *Hinweis: In dieser Aufgabe handelt es sich um eine E-Mail. Insofern musst du darauf achten, dass du einen Empfänger und einen Betreff angibst. Die E-Mail-Adresse kannst du natürlich einfach erfinden. Du schreibst an deinen Cousin/deine Cousine, deswegen kannst du auf förmliche Formulierungen verzichten.*

An: Cozzy@web.co.uk
Betreff: your visit

Hi Sam,
I'm really looking forward to your visit this summer. There's so much to do here that three weeks will seem like a very short time. Are you staying with us all the time or do you want to travel too?
Luckily you can use my sister's room, because she'll be abroad all summer.
If the weather is fine, we can go to the beach and try surfing. Uncle Peter has a lot of surfing equipment, and I've asked him if we can use it. And surprise, surprise, he agreed.

If the weather isn't too good, we could go shopping in Kiel. There is a big shopping mall in the centre. In the evenings we could go to the cinema, and there will be a big party while you are here. Isn't that cool? ☺
If you have any other plans or if there is anything you would like to do while you are here, please email me or give me a ring. I'll organise it.
Oh, and my mum told me to ask you if there is anything we need to know (such as whether you have any food allergies or are a vegetarian). Just let us know.
Before I forget, please tell me when you'll be arriving at Hamburg Airport and what your flight number is, so that we come to pick you up.
See you soon,
Chris *(234 words)*

8. *Hinweis: Bei dieser Aufgabe sollst du deinen Freunden deutlich mitteilen, über welche Art von Geburtstagsüberraschung du dich freuen würdest. Da es dein 18. Geburtstag ist, wird deine Party sicherlich etwas größer ausfallen. Immerhin wirst du volljährig. Da du einen Brief an deine Freunde schreibst, kannst du auf förmliche Wendungen verzichten.*

Hi there,
Wow, you're planning something amazing for my birthday? Great! I just hope it's not going to be anything embarrassing.
Well, don't you remember that I have always wanted to try parachuting? A trip in a hot air balloon would be wonderful too. I'd love to see this place from above. On the other hand, I've been to the United States once and would love to go again, but that's too expensive. Rafting is great as well. I'd also love to learn how to dive. Please don't make me go bungee jumping though. I'd be too scared for that, as you should know.
Please make sure your surprise doesn't clash with my big party, to which you are all invited.
I've rented a stretch limo for the night, and we'll all go clubbing in it. I'm so excited. We'll spend the night cruising from one place to the next. You don't have to worry about accommodation. We can all stay in our wonderful garden house. It's really huge, so all you'll need to bring will be a sleeping bag and a camping mat.
Love, / Best, / See you,
Jonas *(186 words)*

9. *Hinweis: Hier musst du eine E-Mail schreiben, wofür du einen Empfänger und einen Betreff angeben solltest. Du schreibst einem Freund/einer Freundin, den/die du kürzlich über das Internet kennengelernt hast, deswegen kannst du auf förmliche Wendungen verzichten.*

An: Sam@web.co.uk
Betreff: your visit

Dear Sam,
Wow, it's really great that you want to come to Schleswig-Holstein. How exciting! Well, Lübeck's a nice city surrounded by lots of water, so there are millions of things you can do here to stay fit. Most people over here join a sports club or a gym. There are lots of outdoor activities for everyone too, not just for club members. There's a lot of water in and around the town, so you can do water sports like canoeing, sailing, and rowing, or you can go for a run along the river paths. We also like going for a swim in the Baltic Sea. It's only 15 minutes away from Lübeck.
What kind of sports do you do? I could help you to find the right club, or you could just join me and my friends over here. I'm thinking of becoming a member of the big rowing clubs. Maybe we could go together? If you would like to stay at my place, I could ask my parents. We have lots of spare rooms in our house, because my brothers and sisters have already moved out.
I'm really looking forward to meeting you in person soon,
Chris *(204 words)*

10. *Hinweis: Bei dieser Aufgabe musst du in einem Leserbrief deine Meinung äußern. Das heißt, du solltest dir vor dem Schreiben im Klaren sein, wie du zu dem Thema stehst. Baue deine Argumentation geschickt auf und erwähne auch mögliche Gegenargumente. In einem Leserbrief sollte man sich sehr höflich ausdrücken. Verwende daher förmliche Formulierungen.*

(address)
(date)

(editor's address)

Dear Mr James,
I have read the article in which you criticise young people for just sitting in front of their television sets or computer screens. I am sorry, but I do not agree with you. In some cases you may be right, but in my experience

most young people are involved in sports and other activities, or prefer to meet friends rather than spending their time alone in front of the television or computer.

That does not mean I do not watch television at all. I like watching American series, the news, or films and I also use the Internet a lot for homework, to look up things like cinema programmes, or to arrange a meeting with my friends via Facebook. The Internet and television help to keep you up to date and informed about what is going on in the world.

I agree with you that people do get depressed if they use these media too much. If they sit in front of a television all day, they do not leave the house anymore and that isolates them from their friends. Some young people who are Internet addicts sometimes lose touch with reality, and that can be dangerous.

Yours sincerely,

Melissa Oher *(204 words)*

11. ✒ *Hinweis: Bei dieser Aufgabe musst du einen Artikel für einen Wettbewerb verfassen. Die inhaltlichen Aspekte, die erwartet werden, sind schon vorgegeben. Achte darauf, dass du keinen Punkt vergisst. Bei einem Artikel solltest du mit einer Überschrift beginnen, die kurz und knapp den Inhalt wiedergibt und das Interesse des Lesers weckt. Strukturiere deinen Text sinnvoll und benutze Absätze, wenn du einen neuen Gedanken ausführst.*

My dream job – what's the most important thing?

by Tom Meier

Ever since I was a little child, being a farmer has been my dream job. I grew up in a village and my uncle's farm was right next to our house. I was there every day. I had to feed the cows, I helped out in the fields, and I drove the tractor at harvest time. I love working with animals, and being able to work outdoors most of the time is great.

On the one hand you have a lot of responsibility and you are your own boss, but on the other hand it is hard work, and it is not easy to survive today if you just have a small farm. Nevertheless, it is still my dream job.

I am actually not sure exactly how much money a farmer earns and it probably depends on one's position, but that is not the most important thing for me.

Happiness for me is to be outdoors and working with animals. I enjoy thinking up new ideas to make more profit, which I can then invest in better barns or machines. *(191 words)*

12. *Hinweis: Bei dieser Aufgabe sollst du eine E-Mail an die Jobagentur „Global Choices“ schreiben, in der du dich und deine Freundin/deinen Freund vorstellst und dich nach weiteren Informationen über den in der Anzeige angebotenen Job erkundigst. Hier solltest du besonders höfliche Formulierungen verwenden, damit du den Empfänger überzeugen kannst, dass ihr die Richtigen für den Job seid.*

An: amusementpark@santacruz.com
Betreff: application for a job at the amusement park

Dear Sir or Madam,
Having read your advertisement on the Internet, we are writing today for more information about the employment offered.
We are both aged 17 and are looking for a job in the US. We shall be finishing school soon and would like to go abroad before we start studying. We are from Flensburg (Germany), which is near the Danish border.
We want to study English, so we think it would be a good idea for us to spend some time in an English-speaking country to improve our English.
As our first term at university starts in November, we would like to work from the beginning of July until the end of August (this would leave us enough time to travel a little before returning to Germany).
We have already worked as waitresses and cashiers and we would prefer that type of work, but we are also willing to work in other positions.
Could you send us more details with regard to working hours, accommodation and uniforms?
We very much hope that you will consider our application and look forward to hearing from you.
Kind regards,
Lena Langer and Anne Hauptmann *(202 words)*

13. ✎ *Hinweis: Mit dieser E-Mail sollst du einen Vermieter überzeugen, dass du der perfekte Mieter bist. Da du den Vermieter nicht kennst, solltest du besonders höfliche Formulierungen verwenden.*

An: mcallister@edinburgh.uk
Betreff: Flat for rent

Dear Mr McAllister,
Having read in your advertisement that you are looking for a new tenant, I am writing today to ask you to consider offering me your flat.
My name is Karola and I am from the little town Eutin in Northern Germany. I am 18 years old and I have just finished school. I love reading and travelling and so am about to start an internship in Edinburgh at a big publishing company. I shall be working from September on as an assistant to one of the managers.
The office is in the New Town, the centre of Edinburgh, so I would not need a car. I shall probably be working long hours so it would be perfect to have a flat near my office.
I am a quiet, tidy person and enjoy reading in my free time; I also like cooking very much. I am a non-smoker and I do not have any pets.
I shall definitely be earning enough money to pay the rent, as you can see from the enclosed copy of my contract. In addition, my parents would gladly offer a security deposit.
I would be happy to be accepted as your new tenant and I look forward to your answer.
Kind regards,
Karola Green *(215 words)*

Lösungen zum Kompetenzbereich Sprechen/Mediation

Warming up

1. *Hinweis: Wenn du über deine Familie sprechen sollst, kannst du beispielsweise erzählen, ob du Geschwister hast, wie alt diese sind, wo deine Familie wohnt und was deine Eltern beruflich machen. Wenn du die englischen Berufsbezeichnungen nicht kennst, solltest du sie nachschlagen.*

   I have one brother and one sister. My brother Hendrik is nineteen, and my sister Nele is twelve. My brother doesn't live at home anymore; he lives in Neumünster with his girlfriend. There he works as a mechanic.
   Of course, my twelve-year-old sister still lives at home. Although she has got her own room, she always wants to be in mine. She likes to meet my friends, wants to listen to my music, talk, or just hang out. Sometimes she gets on my nerves, but I love her very much.

   Hinweis: Wenn dir zu deiner Familie nichts mehr einfällt, kannst du auch über deine Großeltern, deine Tanten und Onkel oder deine Cousins und Cousinen sprechen. Hier findest du eine alternative Lösungsmöglichkeit:
   I live together with my mother and my father in a small village near Kiel called Ottendorf. I'm an only child. But as my aunt and uncle and some more relatives live in the same village, I often see members of my family, especially my cousin, who is the same age as me. We both play football in the same club and hang out together.
   My parents work in Kiel. My mum works part-time, so she can pick me up after school on her way home. My dad works for a shipping company.

2. *Hinweis: Hast du Haustiere? Wie stehen deine Eltern zu Haustieren? Hier findest du verschiedene Antwortmöglichkeiten ausformuliert.*

   I have got a dog, a golden retriever. His name is Pirate. He's two years old and very wild. I love playing with him in the garden and running around with him outside. I don't like walking him when it is raining, but I still have to do it because he's my pet. I take care of him and I feed him, but my mum takes him to the vet in our car because I can't drive.

Hinweis: Auch wenn du selbst keine Haustiere hast, kannst du darüber sprechen, ob und warum du gerne ein Tier hättest.

I would really like to have a cat. Cats are nice, and you can play with them, but they are also quite independent and can be left alone for a while. My friend has a cat. It jumps on her lap, and she cuddles it. But my mum is allergic to cats so we can't have one. I could have a bird, but I don't think birds are very interesting.

Hinweis: Es gibt auch viele Gründe, die gegen die Anschaffung von Haustieren sprechen. Hier findest du Argumente, mit denen man das begründen kann.

I'm allergic to cats and dogs. If there are cats or dogs around, I start sneezing and my eyes swell. It gets really bad and that's the reason why we can't have a cat or a dog at home.
Pets also need a lot of time and attention. You have to walk your dog whether it's raining or not and whether you want to or not. And you have to take care of your pet, for example by feeding it and cleaning the feeding bowl.
When you have a pet, you can't just go off on holiday whenever you want to. You have to find somebody who can take care of the pet.

3. *Hinweis: Über deine Freizeitaktivitäten solltest du flüssig sprechen können. Schlage wichtige Wörter zu deinen Hobbys nach, wenn du sie nicht ohnehin weißt.*

During the week I don't have that much free time because I have to do my homework and I have to revise for tests. After lunch I usually relax and rest for a while. Then I either chat with my friends or play a computer game. When the weather is nice, I often meet my friends and we go to the city centre in the afternoon.
I like to be active. That's why I do a lot of sports. My favourite sport is handball. Three times a week there are training sessions at my local handball club. If I don't take part regularly, my coach won't allow me to play in the matches at the weekend. I also love swimming. In summer I often go to the beach with my friends.
At the weekends I try to get a good night's sleep and I enjoy getting up late. I like to have a good leisurely breakfast and then I decide what to do.

In summer I might go to the beach if the weather is nice. I love to meet friends and spend time with them.
On Sundays there are often handball matches or tournaments, so I have to get up early. I spend a lot of time in the sports hall, sometimes the whole day.

4. *Hinweis: Das Thema Schule kann sowohl in der sprachpraktischen Prüfung als auch in anderen Prüfungsteilen abgeprüft werden. Du solltest also beispielsweise die Schulfächer benennen können. Wichtige Wörter zu diesem Thema sind in der Beispiellösung fett markiert. Um den Wortschatz gezielt zu üben, kannst du dir eine Mind-Map anlegen und weitere wichtige Wörter zum Wortfeld Schule nachschlagen und eintragen.*

   My favourite **subject** is **PE** because I like to be active. During the school day I have to concentrate all the time, which is exhausting. In the **gym** that's totally different. I don't have to sit still but I can move around, keep my body in shape or compete with my **school mates**. That's fun.
   The subject I don't like is German because we spend a lot of time on **essay writing** and we usually only read one or two books a year. I never know what to write and I'm not sure what I need to do to get good **marks** in the **exams**. Another problem is that I don't get along very well with my German **teacher**. He expects us to listen to his monologues all the time and we never do **group work**.
   If I were the **head teacher**, school would start later. I hate getting up so early. Teenagers need more sleep and time for breakfast. The school day should also be shorter. I sometimes get home very late and I'm often very tired. If I could make the decisions, there would also be less **homework**. **Pupils** would have more influence and the right to take part in important decisions concerning their school.

5. *Hinweis: Zukunftspläne werden in den verschiedenen Teilen deiner Abschlussprüfung oft thematisiert. Überlege dir also gut, was du nach der Schule machen möchtest und wie du das formulieren kannst. Wichtige Wörter zum Thema Beruf sind in der Beispiellösung fett markiert.*

   Having a **job** that is interesting and **well-paid** is one of my goals for the future. But a **high salary** is not the most important thing for me. In the future I also want to travel a lot, get to know different cultures and meet

people in foreign countries. When I'm older, I would like to have a family because I love children.
The first thing I'm going to do after the school-leaving exams is to celebrate with my classmates and all my friends. I've worked so hard for the exams and I'll be extremely happy when they are over.
Then I'll take a rest. I will sleep long, relax and do nothing for a couple of weeks. Of course, I'll spend time with my friends and hang out with them. In September I'll start my **apprenticeship**. I'm sure that I'll like it a lot more than going to school every day because I like to work with my hands. I'm also looking forward to **earning money**. Then I'm less dependent on my parents.

Monologues

Allgemeiner Hinweis: Der monologische Prüfungsteil („Long-term Speaking") dauert pro Prüfling ungefähr vier Minuten. Auf diesen Teil der sprachpraktischen Prüfung kannst du dich sehr gut selbstständig vorbereiten. Am besten nimmst du ein Handy oder ein anderes Gerät, mit dem du deinen Monolog aufnehmen kannst. Lies dir dann eine der Aufgaben durch und versuche, möglichst viel dazu zu sagen. Mach dir keine Sorgen, wenn du am Anfang beim Üben noch sehr zögerlich und mit vielen Pausen sprichst.
Höre dir nun deinen aufgenommenen Monolog an. Achte beim ersten Anhören darauf, ob du inhaltlich alle Fragen beantwortet hast. Lies dir zum Vergleich die Beispiellösung im Buch durch. Höre dir deinen Monolog nun erneut an und überlege dir, welche Wörter oder Formulierungen du gebraucht hättest, um dich flüssiger und genauer auszudrücken. Schlage wichtige Wörter zu den Bildern nach und trage sie in dein Vokabelheft ein. Allgemeine Wendungen, die du immer wieder verwenden kannst, findest du im Kapitel zur sprachpraktischen Prüfung im A4-Band. Wendungen und Konjunktionen, die du immer wieder einsetzen kannst, weil sie nicht auf ein Thema beschränkt sind, sind in der Beispiellösung unterstrichen.
Höre dir nun deinen Monolog noch einmal an und achte darauf, ob du beim Sprechen Grammatikfehler machst. Denkst du daran, bei der 3. Person immer ein -s anzuhängen? Verwendest du das „present progressive", das bei Bildbeschreibungen benötigt wird? Welche Aussprachefehler machst du noch besonders häufig? Wenn dir ein Fehler bewusst ist, wirst du ihn bald vermeiden kön-

nen. Gehe die Aufgabe nun erneut an und nimm deinen Monolog noch einmal auf. Höre dir anschließend die Aufgabe an und vergleiche, was schon besser geworden ist und was du noch üben musst. Wenn du das selbst schwer einschätzen kannst, kannst du auch deine Englischlehrkraft fragen, die dir sicher noch Tipps zur Verbesserung geben kann.

1. *Hinweis: Um die Gefühle der Menschen zu beschreiben, benötigst du Adjektive und Adverbien. In der Beispiellösung sind diese fett markiert. Trage sie in dein Vokabelheft ein, wenn sie dir nicht eingefallen wären. Da du bei Bildbeschreibungen oft Vermutungen über die Situation anstellen musst, kannst du „he or she could/might" oder „probably/maybe/perhaps" gut verwenden.*

   In the foreground of the first picture there is a young woman who has just moved house. She is sitting in her new flat among all the moving boxes and she looks a bit **sceptical**, **exhausted**, and **worried**. In the background you can see a ladder that she might have used for painting the walls of her new place.
   Maybe she is **afraid** of living on her own for the first time in her life. She could also be **worried** about the rent she'll have to pay from now on. She could be about to start unpacking her things so that her new flat will look like a real home. She might call a friend who could help her settle in.
   In the second picture you can see a **young** woman in the foreground. She is standing next to her car and opening the car door. Her parents are standing in the background. They are standing in front of their house, smiling **happily**.
   Their daughter maybe moved out a while ago and has just been back for a visit. They are probably **glad** that their daughter is **independent**. Perhaps she is going to drive back to her own flat after this visit to her parents' house.

   Hinweis: Die letzte Frage dieser Prüfungsaufgabe kannst du sehr frei beantworten. Deswegen findest du dazu hier keine Musterlösung, sondern verschiedene Sätze, die du für deine Antwort verwenden kannst, je nachdem, was auf deine Situation zutrifft.

   I don't know what I want to do when I've finished school. / I haven't decided yet what I want to do when I've finished school. / I'll do an apprenticeship as a … / I'll get work experience at … / I'll stay on at school

to do my A-levels / I'll take a gap year in … / I'll do a voluntary social year … / I'll do a voluntary ecological year …
I don't know when I want to leave home. / I haven't decided yet when I want to move out of my parents' house. / After my apprenticeship I'll move out … / I'll move out of my parents' place right after the final exams are over. / I won't be moving out that soon because my workplace is really close to my home. / I'll move out as soon as I find a flat to share.

2. *Hinweis: Überlege dir, beim Betrachten der Bilder, welche Wörter du benötigst, damit du gut über das Thema sprechen kannst. Schlage wichtige Begriffe nach und trage sie in dein Vokabelheft ein.*

The first picture shows two boys who are probably playing a game on their laptop. In the background, you can see that the curtains have been pulled so that no daylight can get in.
In the second picture, you can see a young boy who is lying on the carpet and holding a mobile phone or a game boy. He is probably also playing some kind of video game. The boy in the picture below looks tired whereas the two boys in the picture above seem to be fascinated.
In my opinion, games on the computer can be very enjoyable. You play to relax and take your mind off problems that you might have at school or with your parents. The ideas behind some computer games are really creative, the pictures are well made, and you can really imagine that you are in that world. Some games require skills which you can practise, for example patience or the ability to react quickly. I know that my classmates are very proud when they have reached the next level or topped their own high scores. There are games which you play together with other people, so you have to communicate or develop strategies. If you play video or computer games, you always have something to talk about with someone who also knows and plays these games.
On the other hand, games such as those can be dangerous. They eat up your time, you forget everything around you, thinking only about the game and which level you are on. That means that you neglect your schoolwork, and then your marks go down. I've heard that some people don't eat or drink when they are playing, so they might even damage their health.

Can parents prevent their children from playing? I'm not sure about that. Sometimes parents can set a time limit, but then their children can just go to their friends' houses to play, like some people I know do. If you don't do sports and if you are bored, you play computer games. One of my classmates is only allowed to play video or computer games for as many hours as he has been outside. That's a nice idea – but what happens when it's raining? You can't go out, so you can't play.

Personally I like playing computer games, but I am only allowed a certain amount of time for that during the week. I play for one hour and then I have to stop, or my parents get cross with me. At the weekend I sometimes play for eight hours, but that's only when we have some kind of party where lots of people all play together against each other. That's great fun. Most of my friends at school have to follow the same rules about playing video or computer games.

3. *Hinweis: Bei diesem Bild ist es wichtig, dass du erkennst, dass der Vogel mit Öl verschmiert ist. Lies dir immer auch die Überschrift zum Bild durch, denn sie gibt dir einen Hinweis auf das Thema, über das du sprechen sollst.*

The picture shows a bird. Someone is holding the bird's wing outstretched, and you can see that its feathers don't look at all normal. They are black and greasy, probably from oil. Environmentalists might have caught the bird so they can try to clean it and save it.

An oil tank might have had a leak, spilling oil into the sea. Not only birds, but also a lot of other animals have probably been affected by this catastrophe. Fish might die because the water is polluted. The bird's feathers are covered in oil and it won't be able to fly any more. Even though some people might try to rescue these animals, their chance of survival is low, and they will suffer. Ecological disasters are generally caused by people but the consequences do not only affect humans: they also hit our environment and the animals that share it with us.

In my opinion, politicians should introduce stricter laws against pollution. Tankers are very often unsafe and can become a problem for the environment. If there were stricter laws against environmentally irresponsible companies, there would no longer be quite so many oil catastrophes.

In addition, everybody should start thinking of the environment and make sure that less oil is needed. In your daily life there are many ways to save energy and protect the environment. Everyone can take small but effective steps. You can reduce plastic rubbish by using paper bags, for example, or you can help the environment by using your bike instead of going by car. You can save water by taking a shorter shower. All these steps not only save the environment, but also reduce your own energy bills.

4. *Hinweis: Hier sollst du zunächst über die Problematik von Tiertransporten sprechen. Anschließend musst du weitere Beispiele dafür finden, dass Tiere oft keine Rechte haben.*

In the photo you can see a lorry full of poultry. The birds are crammed together in small cages. They have very little space and seem to be suffering a lot. They might be on their way to a slaughterhouse to be killed.
One of the problems with all this is that animal transports are carried out all year round. In summer it is very hot outside, and the lorries aren't air-conditioned; the animals aren't given enough to drink either. A lorry can be on the roads for hours or even days until it can unload the frightened, nervous and stressed animals. A lot of them might even die before they reach the slaughterhouse.
People all over the world like eating meat and poultry. But they don't want to pay much for it. Firms want to make the highest possible profit. That's why they try to produce as much meat as possible within a very short time and transport the animals as cheaply as they can. I believe that the real problem is that neither the people who eat meat nor those who produce it feel responsible for the animals.
There are many other examples where animal rights are ignored. Animals are sometimes abused by people just for excitement and fun. Some animals are chased and killed at big-game hunts like tigers in Asia or bears in Russia or in Canada. Other animals, such as elephants, are brutally killed just because poachers want to get the ivory. People sometimes enjoy hunting for sport or catching fish at club fishing events.
Animals are often used in shows, such as dolphins and seals. They have to perform unnatural tricks for the audience. The same happens at the circus. Wild animals are kept in very small cages and instead of being able to enjoy a life in the wild, they have to entertain children and adults.

5. *Hinweis: Über das Thema Kleidung solltest du auch mündlich sprechen können. Kannst du die Kleidungsstücke benennen und beschreiben? Wichtige Wörter zu diesem Thema sind in der Beispiellösung fett markiert.*

The person on the left is wearing the kind of clothes you could wear in your free time. When you go out with friends or when you are at home, you prefer a **casual style** which makes you feel free and easy. And yet you still want to be **trendy** and individual. The young woman in the picture is wearing dungarees – jeans with shoulder straps. But one of the straps is just thrown **casually** over one shoulder like a **fashion accessory**.
On the right you can see a young man in a **suit** and **tie**, which you normally don't wear in your free time – more at work or for a special occasion. If you are employed in an office or in a bank, you might be expected **to dress formally** like that because you represent your firm. Another reason for wearing an **elegant suit** could be a celebration like a wedding or a confirmation.
I prefer the style shown in the first photo. I wear **trendy clothes** because I think fashion is fun and interesting. My style has to include a lot of variety. And it has to be comfortable. I wouldn't like to wear an **uncomfortable suit** every day because I think that's boring. That style would make me feel uneasy, and I would look strange. **Boots** are nicer than old-fashioned black **leather shoes**, which are for people of my parents' age. In a couple of years, I might have to wear a suit, but now I am young and I can make the most of being free to **follow the latest fashion**. I like wearing **cool clothes** because I don't want to be **old-fashioned**. I often go shopping with my friends. We go to the city centre and try on lots of different **outfits**.
However, I hate people who show off with their **expensive designer clothes** and who think nothing is more important than that. I don't like people who are interested in nothing else but wearing **designer labels**. You should go for your own **individual style** and personality. That's why I try to find clothes that suit me and that I personally feel **comfortable** in.

6. *Hinweis: Auch zum Thema Berufswahl solltest du dich mündlich äußern können. Wichtige Wörter zu diesem Thema sind in der Beispiellösung fett markiert.*

In the top left photo there is a young female **firefighter** standing in front of a fire engine somewhere out in the open. She is wearing a firefighter's uniform, boots, and a security helmet. Her arms are crossed. She is smiling and seems to be pleased about something. The photo on the top right shows a young woman sitting at a desk in an **office**, with a computer in front of her. Her right hand is holding a mouse. You can see a printer beside her. She is working in an office as a **clerk** or she might even be an **IT specialist**. The woman's outfit is very elegant. She is wearing a suit, a blouse, and a pearl necklace. She seems to like her job because she is smiling.
In the photo at the bottom a young man in overalls and a white, short-sleeved T-shirt is working on a car, the bonnet of which is open. He seems to be checking whether there is enough oil in the engine. My impression is that he's a professional **car mechanic** because he's so focused on his job.

Hinweis: Du kannst dich bei der zweiten Frage für jeden der drei Berufe entscheiden. Hier findest du daher alle drei Alternativen ausgeführt.

I'd like to be a firefighter. From my early childhood on that has been my **dream job**. In my opinion it is a very interesting and important job. You work in a **team** where people rely on each other. That's real comradeship. You have to be and keep fit so that you can cope with dangerous situations, which may just suddenly come up. You help other people and you can maybe even save lives.
I'd like to work in an office. To my mind this kind of work has a lot of advantages. You don't have to work outdoors so you are not dependent on the weather. You work in a nice office and have your own **workplace**. There is a special dress code, but I enjoy dressing up and wearing trendy and elegant clothes anyway. I like sitting at the computer in my free time, so I'm keen to do that as a **career**, too.
I'd like to work as a **mechanic**. Working inside in an office for eight hours every day would be terrible for me. It's nice to be able to move around, doing different things and I enjoy working with my hands. I'm interested in cars and everything that has to do with them. I want to be able to see

the results of my work. If I repair a car that has broken down, then it will be ready to go out on the road again. I'm responsible for what I do. I like that idea.

Hinweis: Bei der Frage nach deinem Traumberuf kannst du dich völlig frei für einen Beruf deiner Wahl entscheiden. Achte aber darauf, dass du den Beruf und die geforderten Qualifikationen gut genug kennst, um etwas Sinnvolles dazu sagen zu können.

I like computers. That's why my dream job is to work as an **engineer** in the **IT industry**. Developing software programmes and computer games would be one interesting part of that, but tracking down programming errors and **repairing computers** would be a real challenge too. If I wanted to become rich and successful, I could perhaps found and run my own **firm**. I would love my biggest hobby to become my job.
To achieve this goal I'll have to stay on at school after my GCSEs and take some A-levels. Then I'll be able to **study** engineering. After that I'll be fully qualified for my dream job.
My dream job would be to work as a **primary school teacher**. I love children. Playing with my little cousins is great fun, so I often go to my aunt's and uncle's home. In my view teaching is very interesting and full of variety. Seeing the efforts children make and watching them growing up is a great privilege. Besides, teachers earn a reasonable **salary** and have quite a lot of holidays. And, finally, you can easily do this kind of work **part-time**, which is an advantage once you start your own family. For my dream job I'll have to study at university after having taken my A-levels. I'll need a **master's degree** to be allowed to teach, and this will take about five years. After that I'll be given a **work experience placement** at a primary school for eighteen months. Then I'll have to pass one last exam and can **apply for a job** as a teacher.

7. *Hinweis: Hier sollst du die drei Bilder beschreiben und dann begründen, wohin du am liebsten gehen würdest. Außerdem bist du noch aufgefordert, zu erklären, wohin du möchtest, wenn du eine gänzlich freie Wahl hättest, und was du gerne im Ausland tun würdest.*

The top left photo shows a very crowded street full of men. In the background you can see quite high buildings. Some men are joined together to carry a big, heavy boy on their heads, somebody else is walking around

with a big sack on his left shoulder. In the foreground you can see another person pushing a cart. Everybody seems to be in a hurry and is focused on what he or she is doing. The men might be transporting goods, taking them to a market. The scene doesn't look as though it is somewhere in Europe. Perhaps the picture shows a street somewhere in the Middle East or in a country like India because the people don't look like Europeans.
The photo on the right shows a landscape with snow-covered mountains in the background, farm houses in the middle, fir trees in front of them, and lots of snow in the foreground. There is not a single animal to be seen. You get the impression that everything is peaceful and quiet there.
The photo at the bottom is a view of a typical Mediterranean port. In the background there are wooded hills, in front of them some buildings, such as a church with a tower. There are palm trees everywhere. In the foreground a harbour catches your eye. An excursion boat is lying in the calm water, surrounded by some sailing boats. Neither people nor any kind of movement are disturbing what seems to be the perfect silence.
Meeting people from different cultural backgrounds is very interesting for me. I like big, vibrant cities. It's nice to live there for a while and get to know the food, lifestyle and customs of other people. If you live in a large city like the one in the first photo, you can experience a lot of new things. Everything is different and exotic there compared to life in Schleswig-Holstein's cities. That's why I would like to go somewhere far away from home, and the place in the first photo looks just right.

Hinweis: Du kannst dich natürlich auch für das Bild mit der verschneiten Landschaft entscheiden:

The picture on the right really appeals to me, and I'd like to go there. I like the snow-covered landscape, the mountains, and I've always dreamt of being somewhere like that. I don't want to lead a hectic life like the one in that big city of the other picture, and I can't stand large crowds of people around me. I enjoy relaxing and finding some peace and quiet, away from all the trouble and excitement of our daily lives. In the mountains you can learn how to live a simple and quiet life and you can focus on yourself. Added to that, of course, you can do a lot of skiing and snowboarding. The landscape in the picture on the right looks as though I would find a lot of opportunities for winter sports there.

Hinweis: Eine Entscheidung für das Bild eines mediterranen Hafens lässt sich ebenfalls gut begründen:

I would choose the place shown in picture three. I like the Mediterranean. The climate is mild and pleasant and the water is clean and warm. The summers are long, and the winters are normally not as long, cold, and harsh as the ones in Schleswig-Holstein. The food is great, I'm very fond of seafood and I enjoy the variety of fruits and vegetables that are on offer down there. I think that the people are open-minded, friendly, and very hospitable.

Hinweis: Abschließend sollst du erzählen, wohin du gehen würdest, wenn du dich ganz frei entscheiden könntest.

If I were really free to choose, I'd like to go to Australia. It is supposed to be a beautiful country and very special. You can see a lot of different things there and experience a totally different lifestyle. Where and how the Aboriginal people live also interests me a lot. Apart from all that, there are a lot of famous sights to visit, such as the Barrier Reef or Uluru. I'd do a "Work and Travel" programme, where I could earn my own money, so that I wouldn't have to rely on my parents. A few friends of mine have recently been to Australia. They liked it a lot and told me to go there too. I'd really like to do that and see it for myself.

8. *Hinweis: Überlege dir, welche Eigenschaften für diesen Beruf gefordert sind. Kannst du diese auf Englisch benennen? Schlage die Adjektive nach, die du auf Englisch nicht kennst und notiere sie dir in deinem Vokabelheft, denn beschreibende Adjektive sind sowohl in der sprachpraktischen Prüfung als auch beim Schreiben von Texten wichtig. Im folgenden Lösungsbeispiel sind nützliche Adjektive und Adverbien fett markiert.*

I can see two women in the picture, one is sitting behind a counter, the other one is standing in front of it. They are probably in a hotel, in the reception area. It might be a small hotel because there is only one receptionist. She is smiling **politely** at the other woman, who is probably a hotel guest. Perhaps the guest has some questions which the receptionist is trying to answer.
The job of a receptionist is to help hotel guests when they have questions, for example, about checking-out, breakfast, etc. Or if guests want to go on

a sightseeing tour, then the receptionist tells them where they might find one. Sometimes guests would like to have tickets for the cinema or theatre, then the receptionist organizes and books those for them. If something isn't working in a hotel room, the receptionist has to see that it gets repaired as soon as possible. Receptionists also check you in and out, give you your key to the room, and explain when and where you can get breakfast or any other meals.

In my opinion a receptionist has to be a very **friendly** and **outgoing** person. You need to enjoy working with other people, and you ought to be **punctual** and **patient**. When you are in a bad mood, you can't let it show, and the guests should certainly not have to suffer because of that. You need to be **reliable** because sometimes you are **responsible** for cash. Furthermore, you have to be able to work under stress, as sometimes there may be ten guests all needing your help at the same time, and the job can be very **hectic**. I think it can be a great advantage if you know at least two foreign languages because some of your guests might not be able to speak German **fluently**. And that is your job – to make the guests feel **comfortable** and welcome.

I don't think that this would be the job for me. I don't want to be **nice** every day and I don't want to sit in one room all day long. I'd prefer to work outdoors, experiencing nature. I like taking care of plants and seeing how things grow. I'd like to work with my hands and I don't mind if they get dirty. And when I'm in a bad mood, nobody will mind because trees and plants don't care.

9. *Hinweis: Wie behindertengerecht ist deine Schule? Überlege dir, welche Schwierigkeiten ein Mitschüler im Rollstuhl haben könnte.*

In the picture you can see a teenage boy and a girl studying in a school library or at home. In the background, there are bookshelves, which is why I think it might be a school library. The boy is sitting in a wheelchair, and the girl could be a friend of him or his sister. Maybe they are doing their homework or they are revising for a test.

The boy might have various problems at school. If there is no lift, he will find it difficult to get from floor to floor. If some of the doors are not wide enough, he might not be able to get through them with his wheelchair. He will also need toilet facilities suited to his special needs. If every-

thing is built for people who can stand and walk, the person in the wheelchair will be too small to reach things, for example the flush. In the library some of the books might be on the higher shelves, so that he'll need help getting them down. I think it is important that a person in a wheelchair can look after him- or herself and can be as independent as possible.
In addition to these difficulties, the boy possibly has problems making friends because he cannot participate in sports and because a lot of free time activities are more difficult for him. On the other hand, a lot of things teenagers do in their spare time will be no problem for him, such as watching TV, playing computer games or reading books and magazines together with his classmates.
In my opinion it can't be easy for the family to find a new home. They'll need a flat or a house that is suitable for the disabled. A flat would have to be on the ground floor or have a lift and wide doors, a special bathroom; and the boy's room needs to be large enough for him to move around in it on his own. The flat would also need a special kitchen so that he can reach everything and prepare his own breakfast or other meals.

Dialogues

Allgemeiner Hinweis: Auf diesen Teil der sprachpraktischen Prüfung, der ungefähr sechs Minuten dauert, bereitest du dich am besten zusammen mit einer Freundin/einem Freund aus deiner Klasse vor, indem du mit den Aufgaben die Prüfungssituation simulierst. Wie beim Monolog kann es euch auch beim Dialog helfen, wenn ihr euren Dialog aufnehmt. Dann merkt ihr, wo ihr noch besser aufeinander eingehen müsst und ob ihr es schafft, circa sechs Minuten zu sprechen. Die unterstrichenen Konjunktionen und Wendungen in den Beispiellösungen können euch bei allen Dialogthemen weiterhelfen. Gewöhnt euch an, diese Floskeln auch in eure Dialoge einzubauen, damit das Gespräch flüssiger klingt.

1. *Hinweis: Bei diesem Dialog müsst du dich entscheiden, in welches der drei Restaurants du am Samstag mit deinem Freund /deiner Freundin gehen möchtest. Versuche deinen Übungspartner von deinem Vorschlag zu überzeugen. Wenn dir nichts mehr einfällt, was für deinen Vorschlag spricht, kannst du auch erklären, was dir an den anderen Restaurants nicht gefällt.*

Candidate A: Which restaurant would you like to go to on Saturday?

Candidate B: What about Zorbas?

Candidate A: I'm not so keen on Greek food at the moment. We've been there too often. I think it's getting a bit boring.

Candidate B: You're right. I'm a bit fed up too. And the food there is quite expensive. Pizza Palace has reasonable prices. We could go there for a change.

Candidate A: At Pizza Palace there aren't many different pizzas you can choose from.

Candidate B: True, but you can order some other Italian dishes. They also offer a lot of Pasta dishes.

Candidate A: It is very small though. It might be difficult to get a table, especially on a Saturday night.

Candidate B: Hm, Zorbas has got lots of space, you can always find a free table there.

Candidate A: But I'm tired of all the meat you get at Greek restaurants. It's just too much, and they always throw the leftovers away. We all eat too much meat anyway.

Candidate B: And I don't like the loud Greek music they play all the time. It's awful.

Candidate A: You're right. The loud music is terrible. But the music at Pizza Palace is not much better.

Candidate B: Don't forget that Zorbas is quite close. It's only a 10-minute-walk from here, whereas Pizza Palace means half an hour on the bus.

Candidate A: Hm, that's a good reason to choose Zorbas. But the service at the Italian restaurant is a lot better, the waiters are always very friendly and polite. At Zorbas the waiters are always in a hurry and rather unfriendly.

Candidate B: For me the food is more important than the service. Good service doesn't necessarily mean tasty food.

Candidate A: You are right. I don't think we're going to agree on either, are we? So let's think about an alternative.

Candidate B: Have you heard about Best Veggie? It's the new vegetarian restaurant. It's nearby, just around the corner. Sarah has told me that it's a great place.

Candidate A: I've heard about it too. Everything there is freshly made.

CANDIDATE B: Vegetarian food is a lot healthier than meat, by the way.

CANDIDATE A: But I'm not used to vegetarian food. I might not like it. I usually order something with meat in a restaurant. If you go to an Italian or Greek restaurant you always know what to expect. I'm also afraid that eating there is very expensive.

CANDIDATE B: I'm sure we'll find something nice for a reasonable price. They have special offers because they want customers to get to know them. I think the drinks are included in the price.

CANDIDATE A: That sounds interesting.

CANDIDATE B: You should see it this way: nothing ventured, nothing gained. Let's go there and then you can form your own opinion.

CANDIDATE A: Okay, you've convinced me. Let's try something new. I hope we won't regret it. We can meet up at seven and then go there together.

2. *Hinweis: Du planst zusammen mit einem Freund oder einer Freundin einen Strandurlaub, der pro Person 400 Euro kosten darf. Ihr habt die Auswahlmöglichkeiten bereits auf Camping in Dänemark und ein All-inclusive-Angebot auf Mallorca reduziert. Entscheide dich für eine der beiden Möglichkeiten und diskutiere die Vor- und Nachteile der beiden Optionen mit deinem Übungspartner. Am Ende müsst ihr euch auf einen der beiden Vorschläge einigen. Beim Abwägen von verschiedenen Möglichkeiten sind If-Sätze oft sehr praktisch. In diesem Lösungsbeispiel siehst du, wie sie eingesetzt werden können. Versuche auch, zwei bis drei If-Sätze in deinen Dialog einzubauen.*

CANDIDATE A: Hi there. Let's talk about our beach holiday next summer.

CANDIDATE B: Good idea. **If** we book early, we'll get a good price. Which would you prefer – Denmark or Majorca?

CANDIDATE A: I think Denmark is a good choice. We've had such an exhausting year at school that I really need some silence, rest, and time to recover. Relaxing at Denmark's beautiful beaches with the clean air must be great!

CANDIDATE B: You're right. School was really hard. But soon it will all be over, and we need to celebrate! Majorca is the perfect place for that. There are lots of clubs and discos full of young people. By the way, I don't think that there are a lot of clubs or discos you can go to in Denmark. But on Majorca there are tons of places where you can party! I'm also not sure whether there will be any people of our age on holiday in Denmark.

CANDIDATE A: That could be true, but you don't need a club or disco to celebrate and to have fun. **Even if** there are not so many young people holidaying in Denmark, we will definitely meet a few at the campsite. We could have beach parties, that would be nice, wouldn't it? And those long sandy beaches are amazing, not crowded like the ones on Majorca. We might even have the beaches to ourselves **if** we look out for more isolated ones. Majorca's beaches are all full of people.

CANDIDATE B: I agree. **But if** you want to go to the beach, you need beach weather. Think of the last year's summer, which wasn't warm and sunny either in Germany or in Denmark. **If** you go to Majorca, you're guaranteed to get good weather. The sun will be shining every day, and it will always be warm, even in the evening.

CANDIDATE A: Right! But it's a very long way to the beach and there's lots of traffic on the roads. And it might even be too hot in July. **If** you aren't careful, you'll get sunburn or even sunstroke. And I can't sleep at night **if** it's too hot.

CANDIDATE B: I can't either. But all the rooms there are air-conditioned, and you don't have to stay in the sun the whole day long, especially during the first few days. **If** you want to cool down, there's a swimming pool at the hotel. And you can go to the bar and have a cold drink or an ice cream, all for free. Remember? Majorca is an all-inclusive offer. Isn't that a good reason to go there?

CANDIDATE A: That's true. You don't have to pay extra for food and drinks on Majorca, that's an advantage. Denmark is really expensive. But there are long queues everywhere on Majorca, at the bars and in the restaurants, and it will be very crowded and noisy. The staff will probably be stressed and unfriendly.

CANDIDATE B: Maybe. But just imagine us sitting at a table and being served, not having to cook, not having to buy food and drinks. We don't have to do anything at all. That's what I call a real holiday!

CANDIDATE A: You're right. In Denmark we'll have to buy all these things and we'll need a car.

CANDIDATE B: That's it. On Majorca we'll be living in luxury. A bus will take us to the beach, we will have lots of nice food and drinks and a nice big flat with a bathroom and a patio. Added to which, we wouldn't have to squeeze ourselves in a small uncomfortable tent in the rain.

CANDIDATE A: Sharing a tiny and possibly wet tent with you in Denmark doesn't sound like much fun! You've convinced me. Let's hope everything will be just the way you've described it. We'll go to Majorca and enjoy ourselves!

3. *Hinweis: Bei diesem Dialog musst du dich mit deinem Partner über deine Pläne für die Zukunft unterhalten. Du musst dich für eine der drei Auswahlmöglichkeiten entscheiden und deine Entscheidung mit den vorgegebenen Aspekten und eigenen Ideen begründen. Deine Zukunftspläne können sowohl im schriftlichen als auch im sprachpraktischen Teil der Abschlussprüfung drankommen. Überlege dir also rechtzeitig, was du dazu sagen oder darüber schreiben kannst.*

CANDIDATE B: What do you want to do when you've finished school?

CANDIDATE A: Well, I think I want to stay on. My marks are good at the moment, and I actually like learning.

CANDIDATE B: Oh, I wouldn't like that! You know, I'm really fed up with school. I hate getting up early every day. Studying for our final exams is very exhausting, so I'll be ready for a long holiday afterwards. I'm going to get lots of sleep and enjoy the beach.

CANDIDATE A: That's typical of you, a long holiday. But don't you see the opportunities you'll have in the future if you stay on at school? I mean, you learn a lot more and you can specialise in certain subjects. You are quite good at science, aren't you? It would be a great idea for you too. Besides, you can go on holiday every year.

CANDIDATE B: You are right about the holidays, but I would like to get to know other countries, so I need much more than just a few weeks. Maybe I'll go to Australia to work and travel. That would take months!

CANDIDATE A: Yeah, but if you want to work in Australia, you'll need higher qualifications. You will need really good marks in English to find a job.

CANDIDATE B: Like you, you mean? You're the one who should stay on at school. No, honestly I think you're wrong about the marks. I know quite a lot of people who have gone abroad, and their marks were not outstanding either. They still managed. You know, the problem is that I'm not sure what I want to do, maybe I'll go somewhere I've never been before. Then I could learn a completely new language.

CANDIDATE A: What do you have in mind?

CANDIDATE B: Oh, I was thinking about Spanish or Portuguese. For those languages I could go to South America: Bolivia, Peru, Argentina, or Brazil. Just talking about those countries makes me want to go there.

CANDIDATE A: That sounds quite challenging. I'm not as adventurous as you are. I would prefer to stay in Germany. I still don't have any clue what job to choose. There are so many things which interest me. But I'm young, so I'll use the three more years at school to make up my mind.

CANDIDATE B: It's almost the same for me. I can't imagine beginning some kind of training now because I've no idea what kind of job I want. Of course, I'd like to start earning money because I have my dreams and wishes, but if you get stuck in a job you don't like, you'll end up being unhappy. So I'd rather go and see the world.

CANDIDATE A: That's exactly why I want to stay on at school. I think I'll have better chances on the job market if I have higher qualifications. I dream of going to university, you know, maybe becoming a lawyer or a teacher. My parents are very supportive and say that I should take all the time I need.

CANDIDATE B: You a teacher? Funny idea – but why not? Well, my parents aren't very patient. They say that I have exactly one year to make up my mind. They are willing to support me, to a certain extent, that is, maybe in getting my own flat, which I would like to have. But that would mean that I would have to start working very soon. Oh, why is everything so difficult? You have it all figured out, you'll stay on at school next year. I think I need more information about visas and work and travel opportunities before I can decide where to go and what to do.

CANDIDATE A: That sounds reasonable. Good luck.

4. ✍ *Hinweis: Du willst mit einem Freund/einer Freundin eine WG gründen. Überlege dir, ob dir eine Zweier-WG oder eine Vierer-WG lieber wäre und diskutiere mit deinem Übungspartner die Vor- und Nachteile der beiden Vorschläge. Einigt euch am Ende auf eine der Auswahlmöglichkeiten.*

CANDIDATE A: Hi there. I'm really looking forward to moving out from home and leading my own life in my own flat. Let's talk about the two flats we've been offered and decide which one we want to take.

CANDIDATE B: You're right. Time is running out and we must make up our minds soon.

CANDIDATE A: I quite like the idea of the four-room flat. Living together with other people must be very interesting. It broadens your horizon, and you learn a lot from each other.

CANDIDATE B: Sure. But if four people have totally contrary opinions about lifestyles and daily routines, then sharing a flat can become difficult and tiring. Think of cleaning the bathroom or doing the shopping, for example. It's no problem organizing that with just two people. But if there are four, all with different opinions and ideas, this could be difficult.

CANDIDATE A: I agree with you. On the other hand we're young and flexible. And we want to have fun, parties and action. We don't want to lead a boring life in a boring two-room flat, do we? We're interested in meeting and getting to know other people of our own age, and this is our chance to do that. One day, we probably will share a flat with one person for the rest of our lives, but we're still young, we don't have to do that now.

CANDIDATE B: That's true. But consider this: if four people are living together, it might not be easy to get enough rest. Four make much more noise than two. I sometimes need and want peace and silence.

CANDIDATE A: That might be a problem. But don't you think that four adults can show a bit of consideration and agree on a compromise if there are any problems?

CANDIDATE B: Maybe. I just want to be alone once in a while. I need my privacy. And I think you're like that too. If we want to spend time with other people, we can invite friends to our two-room flat. They'll leave after a while and we'll be on our own again.

CANDIDATE A: I suppose it can be a problem, spending part of your life together with other people you don't really know that well and have only met once when they came to apply for the flat sharing.

CANDIDATE B: Another important aspect is that we have been friends for a long time. We know each other quite well. We have the same opinions about many things. If two other people live together with us, we wouldn't know what to expect or whether we can get along with them.

CANDIDATE A: Yes, and it might be really hard to find two people we would actually like to live with. We would have to spend a lot of time and energy interviewing every applicant, and even then it would just be luck. You never know! So you've convinced me. Let's take the two-room flat!

5. *Hinweis: Du möchtest mit deinem Freund oder deiner Freundin eine WG gründen, aber ihr habt nicht genügend Geld für alle abgebildeten Gegenstände. Ihr sollt darüber diskutieren, welche zwei der vier Geräte ihr auf alle Fälle anschaffen wollt.*

CANDIDATE A: Well, what do you think, should we get a microwave? I think that would be a good idea because we can heat up our meals quite quickly and they aren't very expensive.

CANDIDATE B: I agree with you there, but I don't want a microwave because I don't like microwaved meals. I would prefer a washing machine instead, I think we really need it.

CANDIDATE A: No, I don't think so. We can go to a launderette and wash all our clothes there.

CANDIDATE B: But that would be quite expensive in the long run, and I don't want to spend my money on laundry!

CANDIDATE A: Okay, but we could go home to our parents and wash our clothes there. That wouldn't cost much and they'd be happy to see us. Maybe we'd get a nice meal there as well – that would save even more money!

CANDIDATE B: But then I'd have to visit my parents regularly, no thank you. I want to move out to be more independent. That would be impossible if I went home once a week to do my laundry. I tell you what: if you do my laundry at your parents' house, then we can get a microwave for you. How about that?

CANDIDATE A: Hm, okay, that's settled. Now let's see what else we could get. What do you think about getting a computer?

CANDIDATE B: Basically, very useful, but honestly – I'd rather get a laptop. They are much nicer, they look better, and don't take up so much room.

CANDIDATE A: When I said computer, of course I meant a laptop. I really love sitting in front of one and watching series.

CANDIDATE B: But I'm not sure whether we can afford a laptop, especially since we don't really need it.

CANDIDATE A: Just tell me this then: how can I get on the internet without a laptop? I'd like to be able to chat and go on social networks and watch TV online.

CANDIDATE B: You can use your smartphone for all that. So don't tell me you really need a laptop if you have a smartphone.

CANDIDATE A: Now, look, the screen on my smartphone is too small, and it's not cool not having a laptop at home.

CANDIDATE B: Oh, come on, don't be such a snob. We can use the mobile phones for chatting and emailing.

CANDIDATE A: Typing emails on a smartphone is annoying. No, thanks!

CANDIDATE B: It's not your day today, is it? I can see this is getting us nowhere. So what do you think about getting a fridge? That is something we really need to store our food, especially when we get the microwave. Pre-prepared meals and lots of other things really need to be kept in a fridge.

CANDIDATE A: As you know, I'm not a fan of microwave food, but I do agree that we'll need a fridge. Funny that there isn't already a fridge in the flat – I thought it was standard.

CANDIDATE B: You're right, usually it's standard, but the landlord had said that the old fridge was broken and that he'd lower the rent if we buy our own. We definitely need one, and not just to keep your yoghurt cool.

CANDIDATE A: Well, we don't really have much of a choice then, do we? We'll buy a fridge, and you'll get your microwave so that you don't have to do any cooking.

CANDIDATE B: You're so kind – and I promise I'll ask my brother for his old laptop, okay with you?

6. *Hinweis: Ihr habt zu zweit bei einer Verlosung gewonnen und könnt euch für einen der drei angegebenen Preise entscheiden. Überlege dir, welchen du am besten findest und diskutiere mit deinem Übungspartner die Vor- und Nachteile der drei Preise. Es sind bereits Argumente vorgegeben, die im Ge-*

spräch genannt werden können. Am Ende müsst ihr euch für einen der drei Preise entscheiden.

Candidate A: Isn't it great that we've won the raffle? Let's have a closer look at our prize.

Candidate B: Hm, we can either do a mountain climbing course or take a racing bike or € 400 cash. Which do you think we should choose?

Candidate A: Cash is good because we are always short of money, aren't we? It would be € 200 each, that's not bad. And at the moment I'm broke, by the way.

Candidate B: Me too. But if we take the money, we will lose € 400. The mountain climbing course is worth € 800 and the racing bike too. So we would lose € 400. That's a lot.

Candidate A: You're right. € 400 is a lot of money. I quite like racing bikes. I've always wanted to have one, but they were too expensive for me. What about sharing the racing bike and both using it? We could make a special agreement, like I have it one month and you the next.

Candidate B: I don't think that's a good idea. In the summer we would both want to have it, and in the winter nobody wants to ride a racing bike when the weather is bad or when it's snowing. I'm not so keen on racing bikes. You could take it and pay me my share. If you paid me € 40 a month, it would be yours in less than a year.

Candidate A: Sorry, but I don't have the € 40 you want me to pay every month. Remember, I'm broke!

Candidate B: What about putting an ad in the paper and trying to sell the bike for € 600. If it works, each of us will get € 300.

Candidate A: That's not a bad idea. But I've got a different suggestion: Let's take the € 400 and spend it on a big party with all our friends. That would be great fun and an unforgettable event! And we would both profit from the prize.

Candidate B: I agree with you. Doing something together with the money is a great idea. But spending € 400 on a party? Don't you think the mountain climbing course would be great? Both of us could profit from the winnings that way. We would have a lot of fun together. This might become the coolest adventure of our lives!

Candidate A: Aren't you exaggerating a bit? Coolest adventure of our lives? It could be very dangerous. We are not in very good shape and neither of us is very sporty. What's more, we don't know any of the other participants, we don't know the coach and we don't know anything about the company that arranges all this.

CANDIDATE B: Yes, that's true. And for me the time of the course dates are not very convenient. So what shall we do?

CANDIDATE A: As I said before, I need money, you need money. In my opinion the idea of selling the bike was a very good one. The biking season has just started, and lots of people will want to buy a bike at the moment. I'm sure we will get much more than € 400 for it.

CANDIDATE B: You're probably right. So let's take the racing bike!

7. *Hinweis: Bei diesem Dialog musst du dich mit deinem Partner darüber unterhalten, welche Klassenfahrt ihr nach den Prüfungen machen wollt. Diskutiere die Vor- und Nachteile der jeweiligen Alternativen.*

CANDIDATE A: What do you think? Which holiday shall we vote for? I love water, so I would like to go to the North Sea.

CANDIDATE B: What about walking in the Alps? Have you ever done any walking there? I did that two years ago with my older brother, it was a great tour. We saw the sun rise over the mountains and the view was spectacular.

CANDIDATE A: You don't mean to tell me that you got up that early, I can't believe that. I like to have a lie-in, especially when I'm on holiday. Besides, not all our classmates are fit enough to go walking in the Alps for two or three days. I also doubt that the (other) girls in our class would enjoy sleeping in a mountain hut.

CANDIDATE B: Well, we only got up that early once, but still, I really enjoyed walking and I would like to show you and the rest of our class the places we went to.

CANDIDATE A: Thanks, but I honestly don't like walking. It's boring. How would you feel about going to Berlin? We could all stay in a nice hotel. We could go sightseeing in Berlin, there are so many different things to see and do there: Alex, museums, Olympic Stadium – you name it, Berlin has it. We could do so many different things in Berlin. Have you ever been there?

CANDIDATE B: No, I've never been to Berlin and I definitely want to see the capital one day. I'm just not sure whether this is a great idea for a class trip. Think about the costs for a hotel! I think hotels are too expensive for us. And I'd like to see some nature, not just a city.

CANDIDATE A: Hey, what about a camping holiday by the North Sea? We would be out in the open, and going camping is not so expensive.

CANDIDATE B: Yes, and then we'll have a summer like last year's, which was really rainy and wet.

CANDIDATE A: Oh, come on – we're not made of sugar, are we?

CANDIDATE B: No, we aren't. But what would we do there all day long?

CANDIDATE A: We could do a cycling tour or we could play beach volleyball or beach soccer. And if the weather is really terrible, we could always go to the thermal baths.

CANDIDATE B: Okay, so we'll both vote for that suggestion tomorrow. I just hope that we can convince the others as well.

CANDIDATE A: Oh, I'm sure they can be convinced. It is the cheapest alternative, and the people in our class are always short of money.

CANDIDATE B: You're right there. A camping trip is also really easy to organize. Just imagine how difficult it would be to buy train tickets and book all the activities for Berlin.

Mediation

Allgemeiner Hinweis: Der Mediationsteil der sprachpraktischen Prüfung dauert pro Prüfling ungefähr vier Minuten. Lies dir zunächst die Situationsbeschreibung durch. Wenn du allein übst, nimmst du dir anschließend den Mediationsverlauf vor. Lies die englischen Fragen durch und übertrage sie ins Deutsche. Übertrage nun die deutsche Antwort ins Englische. Bearbeite die Aufgaben mündlich und vergleiche das, was du gesagt hast, mit der Beispiellösung. Gehe das gleiche Gespräch nun erneut durch und versuche nun, flüssiger zu antworten. Nur wenn dir das Sprechen am Anfang noch sehr schwer fällt, solltest du dir deine Antworten schriftlich notieren.

Wenn ihr euch zu zweit auf die Prüfung vorbereitet, kann einer die Rolle des Lehrers sowie des deutschen Sprechers übernehmen. Einer stellt die Fragen auf Englisch und vermittelt die deutschen Antworten entweder direkt aus dem Informationsblatt wie in der Prüfung oder aus dem vorgegebenen Mediationsverlauf. Es ist durchaus sinnvoll, eine Übungsaufgabe mehrfach durchzuspielen, denn so gewinnt ihr Routine bei dieser Aufgabenform.

1. *Hinweis: Da bei diesem Prüfungsteil oft nach Öffnungszeiten und Preisen gefragt wird, solltest du dir die Wendungen dazu herausschreiben und sie auswendig lernen. Beachte auch, dass der Lehrer die Fragen oft in der Ich-Form stellt, da er den Austauschschüler spielt. Du änderst das dann beispielsweise zu „mein Freund".*

TEACHER: Do I have to become a member of the rowing club?
DU: **Muss mein Freund Mitglied im Ruderclub werden?**
PARTNER: *Nein, das ist nicht notwendig. Man kann sich die Boote auch gegen Vorlage eines Ausweises ausleihen.*
YOU: **No, that's not necessary. Non-members can also rent boats. They just have to show their ID cards.**
TEACHER: When does the club close in the evening?
DU: **Wann schließt der Club abends?**
PARTNER: *Im Juni und Juli um 21.00 Uhr und im April, Mai, August und September um 19.30 Uhr.*
YOU: **At 9 p.m. in June and July and at 7.30 p.m. in April, May, August and September.**
TEACHER: How much does it cost? Do I have to pay a deposit?
DU: **Wie viel kostet es, sich ein Boot auszuleihen? Wird eine Kaution verlangt?**
PARTNER: *Eine Stunde kostet 10 Euro, drei Stunden kosten 25 Euro und ein ganzer Tag kostet 60 Euro. Für das Boot muss man zudem eine Kaution hinterlegen.*
YOU: It's € 10 for one hour, € 25 for three hours and € 60 for a whole day. You also have to pay a deposit for the boat.
TEACHER: Oh, that's quite expensive! Are there any discounts?
DU: **Gibt es irgendwelche Ermäßigungen?**
PARTNER: *Ja, es gibt eine Ermäßigung für Schüler und Studenten.*
YOU: **There is a reduced tariff for pupils and students.**
TEACHER: Do they only have rowing boats?
DU: **Kann man sich nur Ruderboote ausleihen?**
PARTNER: *Nein, wir haben auch Kanus und Kajaks.*
YOU: **No, they also offer canoes and kayaks.**
TEACHER: What qualifications do I need to use the boats?
DU: **Welche Qualifikation muss man vorweisen, um die Boote benutzen zu dürfen?**

PARTNER: *Man sollte ein Schwimmabzeichen vorweisen können.*
YOU: **You should have a swimming certificate.**
TEACHER: Is there anything else that I need to know?
DU: **Gibt es sonst noch etwas, das man wissen sollte?**
PARTNER: *Schwimmwesten sind verpflichtend.*
YOU: **You have to wear a life jacket.**

2. ✎ *Hinweis: Du musst die deutschen Antworten deines Prüfungspartners nicht wortwörtlich auf Englisch wiedergeben. Es genügt, wenn du den Inhalt übermittelst. Du kannst das oft auch ganz anders formulieren.*

TEACHER: How hot does it have to get for lessons to be cancelled?
DU: **Wie heiß muss es werden, damit Stunden ausfallen können?**
PARTNER: *Es muss um 11 Uhr vormittags im Schatten mindestens 25 Grad warm sein.*
YOU: **It has to be at least 25 °C in the shade at 11 a.m. for lessons to be cancelled.**
TEACHER: Who measures the temperature?
DU: **Wer misst die Temperatur eigentlich?**
PARTNER: *Das macht immer der Hausmeister.*
YOU: **That's done by the caretaker/janitor.**
TEACHER: Oh, and who makes the decision?
DU: **Wer trifft dann die Entscheidung?**
PARTNER: *Die Schulleitung in Absprache mit den anderen Schulen vor Ort.*
YOU: **The headteacher decides together with the headteachers of the other schools here.**
TEACHER: Do all classes then end at the same time?
DU: **Haben dann alle Klassen gleichzeitig aus?**
PARTNER: *Nein, das ist unterschiedlich und hängt von der Klassenstufe ab.*
YOU: **No, that depends which year you're in.**
TEACHER: So, what does it mean for me? I'm in year 10.
DU: **Was bedeutet das dann für einen Schüler der 10. Klasse?**
PARTNER: *Für die 10. Klassen gibt es verkürzten Unterricht. Das heißt, ab der dritten Stunde dauert jede Stunde nur noch 35 Minuten. Der Unterricht endet dann um 12.30 Uhr.*

YOU: **Year 10 has shorter lessons. That means that lessons 3 to 6 only last 35 minutes each. School's out at half past twelve.**

TEACHER: Why do they do it that way for Year 10?

DU: **Warum gibt es diese Regelung für die 10. Klasse?**

PARTNER: *Damit kein Fach besonders vom Unterrichtsausfall betroffen ist.*

YOU: **That way each subject is treated equally. No lessons are cancelled completely.**

3. *Hinweis: Wenn du Uhrzeiten ins Englische überträgst, darfst du „a.m." und „p.m." für vormittags und nachmittags nicht vergessen.*

TEACHER: When does the zoo close today?

DU: **Um wie viel Uhr schließt der Tierpark heute?**

PARTNER: *Der Tierpark schließt im Juli und August um 18.00 Uhr.*

YOU: **In July and August the zoo closes at 6 p.m.**

TEACHER: How much are the tickets for the two of us and our three-year-old daughter?

DU: **Wie viel kosten die Tickets für zwei Erwachsene und ein dreijähriges Kind?**

PARTNER: *Erwachsene zahlen pro Person 7 Euro. Für Kinder unter 4 Jahren ist der Eintritt frei.*

YOU: **The tickets for adults are € 7 per person. Children under four get in for free. So the tickets are € 14 for the two of you.**

TEACHER: How much is a ticket for you? Is there a reduction for schoolchildren?

DU: Wie viel kostet der Eintritt für Schüler?

PARTNER: *Schüler erhalten eine Ermäßigung und zahlen nur 4 Euro.*

YOU: **My ticket costs € 4. It's a reduced price for schoolchildren.**

PARTNER: Our daughter loves polar bears and she would like to see how they are fed. When are they fed?

DU: **Meine Cousine liebt Eisbären und würde gerne die Eisbärfütterung sehen. Wann findet diese statt?**

PARTNER: *Die Fütterung der Eisbären ist um 14.15 Uhr.*

YOU: **The polar bears are fed at 2.15 p.m.**

TEACHER: Are there any animals that our daughter can feed herself?
DU: **Gibt es irgendwelche Tiere, die Kinder selbst füttern dürfen?**
PARTNER: *Ziegen und Schweine dürfen mit Futter, das hier an der Kasse erhältlich ist, gefüttert werden.*
YOU: **You can buy some food here that can be fed to pigs and goats.**
TEACHER: Oh, that's great. Are there any other special attractions for children?
DU: **Gibt es noch weitere besondere Angebote für Kinder?**
PARTNER: *Der Zoo hat einen tollen Spielplatz für Kinder.*
YOU: **The zoo has a fantastic playground for kids.**
TEACHER: We would like to buy our daughter a cuddly toy as a souvenir. Where can we do that?
DU: **Meine Tante und mein Onkel würden ihrer Tochter gerne ein Kuscheltier als Andenken kaufen. Wo können sie das tun?**
PARTNER: *Im Souvenirladen gibt es jede Menge Kuscheltiere für Kinder.*
YOU: **There are lots of cuddly toys in the gift shop.**
TEACHER: Thank you for your help. Let's buy the tickets and see the animals!

4. *Hinweis: Wenn du deinen Lehrer oder deinen Partner in der Prüfung nicht verstehst, weil du zu aufgeregt bist, bitte darum, dass das Gesagte wiederholt wird. Wie du das fragen kannst, steht im Kapitel 4.3 Hilfreiche Wendungen im A4-Band. Lerne passende Nachfragen auswendig, damit du sie in der Prüfung spontan einsetzen kannst.*

TEACHER: How much is a ticket for a teenager?
DU: **Wie viel kostet der Eintritt für Jugendliche?**
PARTNER: *Für Jugendliche bis 14 Jahre kostet der Eintritt 25 Euro, ab 15 Jahren kostet er 31 Euro.*
YOU: **You pay € 25 if you are 14 or younger and € 31 if you are 15 or older.**
TEACHER: Which attractions are included with my ticket? Do I have to pay extra for some of them?

DU: **Welche Fahrgeschäfte kann ich mit meinem Ticket benutzen? Muss ich für manche noch etwas extra bezahlen?**

PARTNER: *Keine Sorge, im Eintrittspreis sind alle Attraktionen und Shows im Hansa-Park enthalten.*

YOU: **They are all included. You don't have to pay anything extra.**

TEACHER: What time does it open on Saturdays?

DU: **Wann öffnet der Park an Samstagen?**

PARTNER: *Der Park ist von März bis Oktober täglich ab 9.00 Uhr geöffnet. Die Fahrattraktionen starten aber erst um 10.00 Uhr.*

YOU: **The Hansa-Park opens at 9 o'clock every day. But the attractions/fairground rides don't start until 10 o'clock.**

TEACHER: How do we get there?

DU: **Wie kommt man zum Hansa-Park?**

PARTNER: *Man kann mit dem PKW, dem Motorrad, dem Bus, dem Zug, dem Fahrrad oder sogar dem Schiff anreisen.*

YOU: **You can get there by car, by motorcycle/motorbike, by bus, by train, by bicycle/bike or even by ship.**

TEACHER: How can we pay for the tickets?

DU: **Wie kann man die Tickets bezahlen?**

PARTNER: *An allen Kassen kann entweder bar oder mit EC- oder Kreditkarte gezahlt werden.*

YOU: **You can either pay cash or by EC or credit card.**

TEACHER: Can we book the tickets in advance?

DU: **Kann man die Tickets im Voraus buchen?**

PARTNER: *Ja, Sie können die Tickets entweder hier buchen oder online im Internet kaufen und ausdrucken.*

YOU: **You can either book the tickets here or you can buy them online and print them out.**

TEACHER: Can we get our money back if it rains?

DU: **Kann man sein Geld zurückbekommen, wenn es regnet?**

PARTNER: *Nein, denn auch bei Regenwetter gibt es viele spannende Unterhaltungsangebote im Trockenen.*

YOU: **That's not possible because there are also a lot of exciting attractions which are indoors/a lot of indoor attractions.**

Schriftlicher Teil

LC Listening Comprehension

LC1 Kiwi experience

Hinweis: Du hörst einen Dialog zwischen Jacob und Emily. Die beiden haben sich länger nicht gesehen. Emily berichtet von den Erfahrungen, die sie in der Zwischenzeit gesammelt hat. Wie die Überschrift bereits erahnen lässt, nahm sie an einem Austauschprogramm teil und reiste nach Neuseeland. Du sollst die sechs Fragen in ca. 1–5 Wörtern und/oder Ziffern beantworten. Nutze die 30 Sekunden, die dir anfangs eingeräumt werden, um die Fragen zu lesen. Dann kannst du während des Hörens die gesuchten Informationen besser herausfiltern.

0. (at a) tourist office
   Hinweis: "First, I learned for exams and then I had a side job at the tourist office" (Z. 2/3)

1. (in) tourist management
   Hinweis: "and then I want to take additional courses in tourist management" (Z. 7/8)

2. (almost) two hours
   Hinweis: "and we were almost two hours late." (Z. 13/14)

3. (by) bus
   Hinweis: "And then I took the bus down to Dunedin" (Z. 15/16)

4. Kiwi (bird)
   Hinweis: "the kiwi is an endangered bird which is still alive." (Z. 23/24)

5. (the) Maori (people)
   Hinweis: "Maori are the native New Zealanders." (Z. 28/29)

6. 165 (photos)
   Hinweis: "I can make a slide show of my 165 favourite pictures." (Z. 39)

LC2 How I found my dream job

Hinweis: Im folgenden Hörtext berichtet Scott davon, wie er über Umwege seinem Traumjob fand. Vorgegeben sind sieben Satzanfänge, die du mithilfe von jeweils ca. 1–5 Wörtern oder Ziffern beenden sollst. Lies dir die Satzanfänge vor dem ersten Hören durch und verschaffe dir einen Überblick. Dann weißt du, worauf du während des Hörens besonders achten sollst. Die gesuchte Antwort kannst du immer eins zu eins dem Hörtext entnehmen, es ist also nicht nötig, dass du in eigenen Worten formulierst. Wichtig ist, dass du deine Antworten anschließend noch einmal liest. Überprüfe dabei, ob sie wirklich sinnvoll und verständlich sind.

0. got some terrible job advice.
   Hinweis: "It was after school that I actually got some really terrible job advice" (Z. 4)

1. was bored (all the time)/was working in a horrible workplace.
   Hinweis: "So, I found myself working in a horrible workplace, I was bored all the time." (Z. 6/7)

2. (sit back and) think again.
   Hinweis: "If the answer is 'because the money is good' or 'I had no better idea', you should sit back and think again." (Z. 12/13)

3. became a travel journalist.
   Hinweis: "or a friend, after years of working for a local newspaper now became a travel journalist." (Z. 16/17)

4. telling them to his (two) nieces.
   Hinweis: "I mean, for me, I love making up stories and telling them to my two nieces." (Z. 22/23)

5. believe in yourself/believe in your (own) dreams.
   Hinweis: "Surround yourself with ambitious and positive people, that makes it so much easier to believe in yourself and in your own dreams then." (Z. 30/31)

6. be a (children's book) writer/be an author.
   ✎ *Hinweis: "I realized I wanted to be a children's book writer." (Z. 32)*

7. writing bedtime stories.
   ✎ *Hinweis: "Now I'm working for a children's book publishing house, writing bedtime stories." (Z. 35/36)*

RC Reading Comprehension

RC1 Unexpected charity

✎ *Hinweis: Viele Unternehmen und Künstler*innen setzen sich für gute Zwecke ein und spenden an bedürftige Menschen. Der Artikel berichtet von verschiedenen wohltätigen Gesten und Aktionen in den USA. Wenn du dir hier unsicher bist, schlag die unbekannten Wörter in deinem Wörterbuch nach. Bei dieser Aufgabe reicht es aus, wenn du deine Antwort in ca. 1–5 Wörtern oder Ziffern notierst. Sie zielt <u>nicht</u> darauf ab, dass du Belege im Text findest und die entsprechenden Sätze herausschreibst. Du sollst das Wesentliche in Stichwörtern wiedergeben.*

0. charitable people and (even) businesses
   ✎ *Hinweis: "we will find that charitable people and even businesses are giving back to communities" (Z. 2/3)*

1. 336 (first-generation students)
   ✎ *Hinweis: "large company, based in California ... Their gifts have allowed 336 first-generation college students to attend university" (Z. 5–8)*

2. 1,400 homes/destroyed homes
   ✎ *Hinweis: "and helped rebuild 1,400 homes after natural disasters." (Z. 8/9)*

3. (free) shoes (for children)
   ✎ *Hinweis: "international shoe company" (Z. 10/11)/"They have chosen to take 16 % of their profits from the shoes they sell to send free shoes to children who are living in poverty." (Z. 13/14)/"the shoes [...] help protect them from infections and injuries" (Z. 15/16)*

4. (in) 2016
   Hinweis: "In 2016 Barack Obama invited him [Chance the Rapper] to the White House in Washington, D.C." (Z. 24/25)

5. (make music for) a good cause/raise money
   Hinweis: "Coming together to make music for a good cause was the idea of several pop music artists . . . in 1979" (Z. 26–28)

6. (to) UNICEF's life-savings programs/charity programs
   Hinweis: "the single raised $4 million for UNICEF's life-saving programs." (Z. 30/31)

RC2 Eating out

Hinweis: Bei dieser Leseverstehensaufgabe geht es um eine Restaurantauswahl. Lies zuerst aufmerksam die Restaurantinformationen (1–7) und die vorgegebenen Situationsbeschreibungen (A–I). Beachte, dass E schon im Beispiel verwendet wurde. Mache dir bewusst, welche Kriterien entscheidend sind – der Preis, das Angebot oder der Tag? Wenn du die passende Beschreibung gefunden hast, trage den Buchstaben in das entsprechende Kästchen ein. Es bleibt eine Beschreibung übrig.

0. **E**
   Hinweis: "This new restaurant has different types of live music every night except Sundays" (Z. 5/6)

1. **G**
   Hinweis: "In summer enjoy your meal in the beautiful garden." (Z. 10)

2. **F**
   Hinweis: "We recommend the pasta and seafood." (Z. 16/17)

3. **H**
   Hinweis: "you can have breakfast at any time you like during the day" (Z. 21)

4. **B**
   Hinweis: "This pretty restaurant serves healthy food" (Z. 24)/ "Food is bought from local producers whenever possible." (Z. 26/27)

5. **A**
   Hinweis: "dinner can be expensive." (Z. 31)

6. **I**
   Hinweis: "Speed and quality are important here, and the prices aren't bad either." (Z. 36/37)/"all on the table in super quick time" (Z. 36)

7. **C**
   Hinweis: "They only do desserts" (Z. 41)

W Writing

W International Cuisine Day

*Hinweis: Deine Schule hat vor einigen Wochen einen „International Cuisine Day" veranstaltet, an dem Essen aus aller Welt zubereitet und verkauft wurde. Den Erlös habt ihr gespendet. Auch du hast an diesem Tag mitgewirkt und berichtest deinem englischen Freund bzw. deiner englischen Freundin in einer E-Mail davon. Notiere dir vorerst deine Antwortideen zu den vier Fragen. Warum warst du an dem Projekt interessiert? Wie sah dein Mitwirken und das deiner Mitschüler*innen aus? Wem wird der Erlös zugutekommen? Wie habt ihr im Nachhinein auf den Aktionstag aufmerksam gemacht?*
Wenn du deine Antworten in Stichpunkten notiert hast, schreibe die E-Mail. Vergiss Anrede und Einleitung nicht und wähle eine geeignete Grußformel am Schluss. Achte darauf, dass du nicht zu formell formulierst. Ganz wichtig ist, dass du in der Vergangenheit schreibst, da die Veranstaltung bereits stattgefunden hat. Führe deine Stichpunkte aus, sodass dein Freund bzw. deine Freundin einen guten Eindruck von dem Aktionstag erhält und vielleicht sogar angeregt wird, einen ebensolchen auf die Beine zu stellen. Du sollst ungefähr 180 Wörter schreiben, wobei der folgende Lösungsvorschlag etwas länger ist, um dir ein paar Anregungen zu geben.

Dear Phil,

How are you and how is school? I cannot complain. We recently had a great event at school – the "International Cuisine Day". Some of my friends and I volunteered to support the project. When I heard of the project I was very interested in it. As you know, I love cooking and I also love different kinds of food. Additionally, it is always a good idea to help others.

First, we collected recipes and decided on the food we wanted to prepare. In groups we prepared and sold dishes from different countries. My group represented Indian cuisine, that's why we cooked a spicy vegetable curry. In the afternoon our families, friends and other hungry people from town visited our school, and the feast began.

At the end of the day we could proudly announce a profit of € 2,000. We donated the money to an organization which helps children in Ghana. The organization enables children to attend school and provides them with food and medicine. To draw attention to our project, we filmed the initiative and a friend of mine created a documentary showing the highlights of that day. He uploaded it on YouTube and our school's website. Everyone enjoyed that day and I hope that you'll be able to join it if it is repeated next year.

Best wishes,

Laura *(223 words)*

Sprachpraktische Prüfung

Monologue

Hinweis: In den folgenden Lösungsvorschlägen sind nützliche Formulierungen, die du bei fast jedem Thema verwenden kannst, unterstrichen. In Kapitel 4.3 des Trainingsbandes findest du weitere solche hilfreiche Wendungen.

Protecting the planet

1. *Hinweis: Klimawandel ist ein bedeutsames Thema, das oft Teil der sprachpraktischen Prüfung ist. Nach der Beschreibung der Bilder schaffst du optimalerweise schon eine kurze Überleitung zwischen der Bildbeschreibung und der zweiten Aufgabe.*

   In the first picture I can see a harbor. There is a cargo ship and the chimney of a factory in the background, a crane on the riverbank on the right and metal parts on the river side on the left. It's probably early in the morning because it looks like the sun is rising behind the factory skyline.
   The second picture shows a polar bear on a sheet of floating ice surrounded by nothing but sea and sky. Only a narrow stripe of light lets us see where the water ends and the sky begins. The polar bear is all alone on the small piece of ice and has almost no space to move on it.
   Whereas the first picture shows how we humans pollute the environment, the second picture visualizes how the climate is changing and makes us aware of the consequences.

2. *Hinweis: Überlege dir für diese Aufgabe, inwiefern unser tägliches Handeln einen Effekt auf die Umwelt hat, und nenne Beispiele. Mögliche Beispiele sind die Umweltverschmutzung durch Fabriken und unnötige Plastikverpackungen. Natürlich kannst du auch andere Beispiele anbringen, wie Schadstoffausstoß von Autos, übermäßiger Fleischkonsum o. Ä.*

   Every one of us has a strong impact on the environment every day. First of all, all goods we use need to be produced, and the production uses resources and pollutes the environment. Every piece of clothing, every smartphone and every plastic bottle therefore has an effect on the environment. Moreover, plastic is a big problem in general. We often use plastic bags and buy things that are wrapped in plastic, for example food or electronic devices.

So the decisions we make daily leave a mark on our carbon emission account, commonly known as the carbon footprint: The bigger your footprint, the more of a negative effect you have on the environment.

3. *Hinweis: Nun stellst du Maßnahmen vor, die du ergreifen kannst, um unseren Planeten zu schützen. Bleibe hierbei ganz bei dir und deiner Umgebung. Was unternimmst du, um die Erde zu schützen?*

As every decision we make somehow affects the environment, everyone can do something to help protect the planet. I try to use as little electricity as possible and turn off my phone at night and while I'm at school. I make sure that it's not in standby mode because that uses up a lot of energy too. Furthermore, everyone in my family uses cloth bags instead of plastic ones for fruit and vegetables in order to avoid waste. Additionally, we mostly buy fresh and local. In this way, we avoid buying food that has travelled a long way. We also only own one car which we use as rarely as possible. My father goes to work by train and my mother uses the bicycle in summer. My brother and I usually walk to school, sometimes we go by bike. Finally, we don't travel long distances. For our last holiday my family and I went to Bavaria by train. We went hiking, rafting and cycling there. I didn't feel I was missing out on anything.
In general, I try to help protect the planet in my everyday life. I'm convinced that everyone has the chance to do something and it doesn't take much effort.

Fashion – second-hand or new?

1. *Hinweis: Betrachte die beiden Bilder und beschreibe sie nacheinander. Die Überschrift gibt dir Aufschluss darüber, dass es um das Thema „gebrauchte oder neue Mode" geht.*

The first picture shows a young woman who's looking through different pieces of clothing hanging from racks. She's got long dark hair and is wearing a knitted hat, a scarf around her neck and a woolen coat. She's most likely in a clothes shop or at a flea market. She's smiling and seems to be satisfied. Maybe she found a pullover that matches her outfit.
In the second picture I can see three young women. They've all got long hair. The woman in the foreground is wearing a straw hat and the woman on the right is pointing at an outfit in a shop window to their right. The

outfit must have caught her attention because she's showing it to her friends and it looks like they're about to go inside the shop. I think they probably love to go shopping.

2. *Hinweis: Wie sehen deine Shopping-Gewohnheiten aus? Wie gern, wie häufig und wo gehst du Kleidung kaufen?*

I love fashion and I always keep up with the latest trends. In fact, I wander around shops downtown or go to the big shopping malls nearby quite often. Every other month my aunt and I check out different outlet stores in the vicinity. I certainly can't afford pricy clothing and designer labels, but sometimes I get lucky and find shoes or a handbag on sale. I also sometimes check out second-hand shops because my mum prefers them. She finds quite a few stylish clothes there and has a very good fashion sense. I've already bought one or two outfits in a second-hand shop for myself. The good thing about second-hand shops is that sometimes you can find used clothes which you could never afford in regular shops.

3. *Hinweis: Welche Vor- und Nachteile hat das Kaufen von Second-Hand Mode? Bringe Argumente dafür und dagegen strukturiert vor und fasse am Ende deine Position noch einmal kurz zusammen.*

As I've already mentioned, one of the advantages of second-hand shopping is the price. You can buy designer fashion for less money and, if you're lucky, make a real bargain. Sometimes you have a certain piece of clothing in mind but can't find it in any store because it's not trendy right now. That's when a second-hand shop might be a good place to visit. My last argument in favor of second-hand clothes is their eco-friendliness: if you reuse clothes you can help protect the environment.

On the other hand, there are also arguments against shopping in second-hand stores. Clothing sold there is mostly only available in one size. Imagine finding a great blouse but it's too small – that can be a real disappointment. You should also keep in mind that someone else has worn the clothes before, so they might have stains.

To conclude, I would say that it depends on your individual taste whether or not you buy clothes in second-hand stores. Personally, I prefer buying new clothes, but I appreciate some advantages of second-hand shops.

Different ways of expressing yourself

1. *Hinweis: Beschreibe, wie der Graffitisprayer und der Mann am Schreibtisch aussehen und was sie machen. Vergiss nicht, das* present progressive *zu benutzen, z. B. „He's spraying".*

   In the first picture, I can see a person who's spraying a graffito on a stone wall. The person is wearing a hoodie and the hood is covering the face, so I can only guess the person's sex and age, but I think it's a young man. He's probably spraying the graffito illegally and doesn't want to risk giving away his identity. The man is just spraying the sharp teeth of a monster face. Next to the man, there are two more spray cans.
   The second picture shows a man writing on a paper. The man is approximately thirty years old, is wearing glasses and has got a beard. He's very focused on his work. To his left and right there are two piles of books. There is also a laptop right in front of him. He's sitting at a large table in what looks like a library and it appears that he's not fully satisfied with his work so far because there are lots of pieces of crumpled paper lying all over the table. Maybe the man is an author writing a novel.

2. *Hinweis: Nach dem Beschreiben der Bilder sollst du erklären, wie du deine Fantasie einsetzt, um deinen Ideen und Gefühlen Ausdruck zu verleihen. Du kannst auch von Freundinnen oder Freunden erzählen, die ihre Gefühle auf kreative Art ausdrücken. Mögliche Beispiele sind fotografieren, Videos erstellen, zeichnen, Tagebuch schreiben, Musik machen, basteln etc. Diese Aufgabenstellung musst du vielleicht zweimal lesen, um sie ganz zu verstehen. Wenn dir in der Prüfung eine Aufgabe nicht klar sein sollte, frage ruhig nach, ob du sie richtig verstanden hast ("Excuse me, I'm not sure if I understood the task correctly ..."). Dafür werden dir keine Punkte abgezogen.*

   Where others might write a diary entry, I play music to express my ideas and feelings. Interacting with others, the power of nature and so on – there are numerous things which impress and inspire me daily. That's when I grab my guitar in order to set my feelings to music. Every now and then I also write a song. Since I'm a positive and optimistic person, most of my songs are very happy and light. I mostly keep these songs to myself and rarely share them with anyone. Certainly, there are situations where I play the guitar with my friends or family, but normally it's only cover songs or the personal birthday songs I write for friends. In these songs, I portray the friends' characters. They are the only songs I like to share with others, sometimes even on social media.

3. ✎ *Hinweis: Findest du, dass Fächer wie Kunst, Musik oder Darstellen und Gestalten an der Schule eine angemessene Rolle einnehmen? Sage deine Meinung dazu und begründe sie.*

I am of the opinion that subjects like art, music or drama don't need to play a more important role at school. Four of my lessons a week are such creative classes. Together with my two P.E. lessons, these have always been the classes where I could relax and wasn't under any pressure. Here, the focus lies more on the individual person and not on achievements and results, so I think they are very important.
However, during such lessons you might not find the right atmosphere to really express yourself, whereas after school you get the chance to meet people who are interested in the same things you are. For the last three years I've been part of our school's drama group. We mainly meet after class and that has been a great experience. I assume that when you're interested in the field of art, there's always time in the afternoon and evening to be creative. Moreover, you must bear in mind that subjects like maths and languages are more important to pass final examinations and find a job. Therefore, I think that creative subjects don't need to become more prominent at school.

Dialogue

*Hinweis: Es sollte niemand zu schnell nachgeben; wenn ihr unterschiedlicher Meinung seid, habt ihr den Ansporn, eure*n Partner*in zu überzeugen. So haltet ihr das Gespräch automatisch am Laufen. Achtet darauf, dass ihr einander gut zuhört und aufeinander eingeht.*

Presents for your host family

Hinweis: Gern würdet ihr eurer englischen Gastfamilie typisch deutsche Mitbringsel schenken. Sprecht über alle Vorschläge und überlegt, welche Geschenke für die Eltern, die 10-jährige Tochter und den 15-jährigen Sohn sinnvoll sind. Wichtig ist, dass ihr euch auf drei Geschenke einigt, sodass alle etwas bekommen.

Candidate A: Hello Samira, how are you?

Candidate B: Hi Robin, I'm looking forward to our trip to Bristol next week. Don't you think it would be nice to bring along some presents for our friends' families?

Candidate A: Yes, that's a good idea, Samira. So we need presents for Tim, who's our age, for his 10-year-old sister Tina and for the parents.

Candidate B: How about souvenirs which are typical of northern Germany?

Candidate A: You mean like cups saying "ebb and flow" or a calendar with lighthouses?

Candidate B: These are fun ideas, but such cups are always a bit kitsch, don't you think? And it's summertime, we shouldn't buy a calendar starting in January.

Candidate A: You've got a point there. Do you have any other ideas?

Candidate B: Do you know if Tim is a soccer fan? We could buy him a soccer jersey of HSV or St. Pauli. What's your opinion on that?

Candidate A: He's a huge soccer fan, but he's only interested in the Premier League and doesn't really know German soccer teams besides Bayern Munich and the BVB. And I'm definitely not buying any of their jerseys.

Candidate B: Alright, I see. Do you think he would like some German music? We could create a playlist with some cool German songs.

Candidate A: I'm not sure about that. I have no idea what kind of music he likes and he won't be able to understand the lyrics. But I know that he loves sweets, so let's keep that in mind.

Candidate B: Oh, great, so we could get him some marzipan and German chocolate. And, speaking of which, I remember that his parents love cooking. How do you feel about a cooking book?

Candidate A: You mean one with typical German recipes like Schnitzel and Labskaus? I doubt that they'd use it. They mainly cook healthy food and only eat meat once or twice a week.

Candidate B: You're absolutely right. But my mother recently got a cooking book with healthy, fresh and seasonal German food. It's called *German Cooking Today*. I think that would make a great present.

Candidate A: That's a good idea. And it's written in English? Remember, our host parents' German isn't the best.

Candidate B: Funnily enough, it's bilingual. From my point of view, this is a perfect present.

Candidate A: I agree with you. Now we still need a present for Tina. As far as I know, she loves doing puzzles. We could get her a puzzle showing the beautiful panorama of Hamburg at night.

Candidate B: I am sure she'd like that!

Candidate A: OK. Shall we meet downtown tomorrow to buy the gifts? By then I'll know where we can get the cooking book.

Candidate B: Alright, thanks! And marzipan, chocolate and the puzzle shouldn't be hard to find.

Candidate A: That sounds like a fantastic plan. See you tomorrow.

Candidate B: Bye, have a good day.

Greatest sports event

Candidate A: Good morning Sam. How are you?

Candidate B: Hello Leonard. I'm doing well, what about you?

Candidate A: My muscles are a bit sore after last night's soccer practice.

Candidate B: I can imagine. Do you want to hear my idea for our trip to the greatest sports event in the world?

Candidate A: Sure, what is it?

Candidate B: I'm thinking about a trip to Austria next summer. I'd love to see the best eSports players at a festival there. I watched a video yesterday, and it looks amazing.

Candidate A: I'm sorry, but I'm not that much into video games. I can't imagine spending several days at a gaming festival.

Candidate B: Too bad. And I thought I had finally found our event.

Candidate A: Why don't we go to the Olympic Games? There we'll get the chance to watch all kinds of sports.

Candidate B: No chance, the next Olympic Games are in Tokyo and that's too far away and too expensive.

Candidate A: I understand. My big dream has always been the NFL Super Bowl in the US. My aunt lives in Florida. We could stay at her place and we'd only have to pay the flights.

Candidate B: That's a good idea, but then I've never played football nor watched a game. Do you like darts? The World Darts Championship takes place in London.

Candidate A: Yes, I do. But darts is me and my dad's thing and I promised him that we'd see the World Darts Championship together one day.

Candidate B: I see. And what about our dream that we'd go to the Soccer World Cup at least once in our lives?

Candidate A: Yes, I remember that we had agreed on that. But there will be no Soccer World Cup soon …

Candidate B: Hm, how about handball? I love watching handball.

Candidate A: So do I. I used to play in the school's handball team, too.

Candidate B: The EHF Champion's League takes place in Germany. By next year I should have my driver's license, so I could drive there.

Candidate A: That sounds great!

Candidate B: How about this: we'll definitely go to the EHF Champion's League next year and keep in mind the Soccer World Cup for the future.

Candidate A: That sounds perfect. You'd better practice for your driving test.

Candidate B: I will, I promise. Let's go to class.

Learn a new language

Candidate A: Hi Helena, how are you?

Candidate B: Hello Jonas, I'm fine, thanks. What have you been up to lately?

Candidate A: I was on holiday in Vietnam. It's a great country, I tell you. I'm thinking about spending my gap year there and I would like to learn Vietnamese.

Candidate B: That sounds exciting. I'll start learning Russian soon because of my relatives who live in Russia. But it's probably pretty tough.

Candidate A: I well believe it. And how will you learn Russian?

Candidate B: I've registered for a 12-week language class which will begin next week. We'll meet twice a week for one and a half hours.

Candidate A: How much does it cost and how many students are in your class?

Candidate B: It costs € 180 and I think about 15 students will attend.

Candidate A: € 180 – that means you pay € 60 a month. That's quite a lot. I couldn't afford this. Furthermore, I can't imagine that learning a language in a big group is effective.

Candidate B: I see it differently. I think it's fun and I look forward to meeting new people in my language class. And going abroad, for example, costs much more.

Candidate A: You're right. Going abroad for three weeks costs € 500!

Candidate B: Yes, unfortunately, that's very expensive. Although I'm sure that if you learn a language in the country where it's spoken you make the best progress.

Candidate A: Yes, absolutely, but € 500 is out of the question. Have you ever tried one of those language apps? It's said to be easy and fun.

Candidate B: Yes, I used an app to learn some Danish before my summer trip. After a little while I was able to introduce myself, but I didn't understand the Danish people who answered me once I was in Copenhagen.

Candidate A: How much did the app cost?

Candidate B: Usually you pay € 5,99 a month.

Candidate A: That's a cheap alternative and you stay flexible. But on the other hand, you don't interact with others and you haven't got the chance to communicate.

Candidate B: That's why I decided on a language class. On top of that, I'll receive a certificate at the end of my course, which always leaves a good impression when you apply for an apprenticeship or a job.

Candidate A: That's a good point.

Candidate B: Wait a moment! I've got an idea. I saw a poster in the library advertizing a tandem party.

Candidate A: You mean a get-together where you can find a communication partner from abroad?

Candidate B: Exactly. Maybe you'll get lucky there and find a native speaker from Vietnam who's nice. That way you might make a new friend, you get to talk in a foreign language, and I bet you'll have a lot of fun.

Candidate A: And I wouldn't have to pay anything. This way I could save my money for my gap year. Thank you so much! I'll have a look right away.

Candidate B: I'm glad I could help you. You're welcome. Have a nice day and good luck!

Mediation

Hinweis: Höre gut zu und scheue dich nicht nachzufragen, wenn du etwas nicht verstanden hast. Achte dabei darauf, wen du in welcher Sprache ansprichst. Du musst bei der Mediation nicht jedes einzelne Wort in die jeweils andere Sprache übersetzen, auch mit Umschreibungen lassen sich viele Auskünfte erteilen.

Boßeln

Lehrkraft (= Engländer): Excuse me, I'd like to know something about this activity. What exactly are they doing?

Du: Entschuldigen Sie bitte. Dieses Ehepaar würde gerne etwas über diesen Sport erfahren. Was machen Sie hier genau?

Mitprüfling (= Veranstalter): *Das ist ein Volkssport aus Norddeutschland namens „Boßeln". Man spielt es in Parks oder auf wenig befahrenen Landstraßen.*

Du: They're playing a sport which is popular in northern Germany. It's called "Boßeln" and you play it in parks or on rural roads without much traffic.

Lehrkraft: Never heard of it. What are the rules of this game?

Du: Was sind denn die Spielregeln?

Mitprüfling: *Man muss versuchen, die Kugel mit weniger Würfen als die gegnerische Mannschaft ins Ziel zu bringen. Der Spaß steht im Vordergrund.*

Du: You must get the ball into the goal with less shots than the opposing team. This game is all about fun.

Lehrkraft: That sounds like fun. Why are they pulling a wagon?

Du: Warum ziehen die Teams einen Bollerwagen?

Mitprüfling: *Der Bollerwagen dient dem Transport von Verpflegung und Ausrüstung, wie zum Beispiel einem Kescher für den Fall, dass die Kugel ins Wasser rollt.*

Du: The wagon is for food and drinks and the equipment, for instance a net which is used if the ball rolls into the water.

Lehrkraft: I see. Who can take part in this sport?

Du: **Und wer kann bei diesem Sport mitmachen?**

Mitprüfling: *Boßeln ist für alle Altersgruppen geeignet, auch für Kinder. Sie spielen mit einer leichteren Kugel und ihre Strecke ist kürzer.*

Du: **"Boßeln" is for all ages and children can play it, too. They use a lighter ball and have a shorter distance.**

Lehrkraft: Great. When can you do this sport?

Du: **Wann kann dieser Sport ausgeübt werden?**

Mitprüfling: *Boßeln kann man das ganze Jahr über bei jedem Wetter. Da draußen gespielt wird, ist das einzig Wichtige das Tageslicht.*

Du: **You can play this sport year round, regardless of the weather. The only thing that is necessary is daylight since it's played outside.**

Lehrkraft: That makes sense. How much does it cost to play?

Du: **Wie viel kostet es?**

Mitprüfling: *Es kostet 20 € pro Person, inklusive Einweisung. Kinder bis 14 Jahren zahlen die Hälfte.*

Du: **It costs € 20 per person, including the instruction. Children up to the age of 14 pay half price.**

Lehrkraft: OK. I think our grandchildren would love to do that. How can we contact you?

Du: **Sie glauben, dass ihre Enkelkinder das Boßeln gerne mögen würden und möchten wissen, wie sie Sie kontaktieren können.**

Mitprüfling: *Hier ist meine Visitenkarte mit Telefonnummer, E-Mail-Adresse und Website.*

Du: **This is the organizer's card with his phone number, e-mail address and website.**

Lehrkraft: OK, we'll talk to our grandchildren. Thank you so much for your help.

Bauernhof-Eis

Lehrkraft (= englische Familie): Excuse me, we'd like to know something about this café. What kind of café is it?

Du: **Diese Familie würde gerne etwas über dieses Café erfahren. Welche Art von Café ist es?**

Mitprüfling (= Caféinhaber): *Das Hofcafé wird seit 2014 von der Familie Stuck geführt und ist bekannt für das leckere Eis.*

Du: **This café has been managed by the family Stuck since 2014. It's known for its delicious ice cream.**

Lehrkraft: I see. What can you tell me about your ice cream?

Du: **Was gibt es über das Eis zu sagen?**

Mitprüfling: *Das Eis wird aus frischer Milch oder Sahne von unserem eigenen Hof hergestellt. Die Zutaten kommen aus dem Garten oder der Region.*

Du: **They make the ice cream from the milk or cream they produce on their own farm. The ingredients either come from the garden or the region.**

Lehrkraft: Yummy. How many different sorts of ice cream do you sell?

Du: **Wie viele verschiedene Sorten Eis verkaufen Sie?**

Mitprüfling: *Wir verkaufen über 100 verschiedene Variationen, wie zum Beispiel Senf- oder Knoblauch-Eis. Wir bieten besondere Sommer- und Wintersorten an.*

Du: **They sell over 100 different variations of ice cream, for example mustard or garlic ice cream. There are special summer and winter sorts.**

Lehrkraft: That's amazing. What else can we do here?

Du: **Die Familie findet das großartig. Sie möchten außerdem wissen, was sie hier sonst noch machen können.**

Mitprüfling: *Man kann bei der Herstellung zuschauen oder an einer Verkostung von 30 verschiedenen Eissorten teilnehmen.*

Du: **You can watch how the ice cream is made or take part in a tasting of 30 different kinds of ice cream.**

Lehrkraft: Oh, that would be fun. How much is it?

Du: **Wie viel kostet das denn?**

Mitprüfling: *Kinder bis 5 Jahre haben freien Eintritt. Kinder und Jugendliche von 6 bis 17 Jahren zahlen 7 €, Erwachsene 14,50 €.*

Du: **Children up to the age of 5 don't have to pay anything. Children and teenagers who are 6 to 17 pay € 7, for adults it's € 14.50.**

Lehrkraft: That's quite reasonable. How often do these tastings take place?

Du: **Wie häufig finden die Verkostungen statt?**

Mitprüfling: *Sie finden mindestens zweimal im Monat statt. Die Terminübersicht ist am besten im Internet zu finden.*

Du: **Tastings are offered at least twice a month. The best way to check out the dates for the tastings is online.**

Lehrkraft: Good idea. We will have a look. What else do we need to know?

Du: **Gibt es noch mehr, das die Familie wissen sollte?**

Mitprüfling: *Die Teilnahme ist nur nach Voranmeldung möglich. Unverträglichkeiten müssen unbedingt vorher angegeben werden.*

Du: **You can only participate in a tasting if you register in advance. In case you suffer from a food intolerance, you should let them know in advance, too.**

Lehrkraft: Good to know. Thank you so much for your help.

Kunstausstellung

Lehrkraft (= Austauschschülerin): Excuse me, I've just read your flyer and would like to know more about your gallery showing this collection of funny paintings and pieces of art.

Du: **Entschuldigen Sie, meine Austauschschülerin würde gern mehr über Ihre Galerie und die Sammlung lustiger Bilder und Kunstwerke erfahren.**

Mitprüfling (= Museumsmitarbeiter): *Die Ausstellung bietet besondere Werke zu Momenten der Weltgeschichte. Es handelt sich um Bilder und Skulpturen mit Entenmotiven und ist eine Mischung aus Comic und Kunst.*

Du: **The exhibition shows special pieces of art focusing on different moments in world history. You can see pictures and sculptures with duck motives. It's a mixture of cartoons and art.**

Lehrkraft: Wow, that sounds like fun. But what exactly is the role of the ducks here?

Du: **Welche Rolle spielen denn die Enten?**

Mitprüfling: *Berühmte Personen der Geschichte, Kultur und Kunst werden durch die beliebtesten Enten der Welt dargestellt: Donald Duck und Co.*

Du: **Famous people from history, culture and art are represented by the most popular ducks of the world: Donald Duck and so on.**

Lehrkraft: That sounds great. What else might be important to know?

Du: **Gibt es noch weitere wichtige Informationen?**

Mitprüfling: *Die Ausstellung wandert durch diverse Städte. In jeder Stadt werden andere Werke gezeigt, zum Beispiel das jeweilige Wahrzeichen der Stadt.*

Du: **This gallery travels through various cities. In every city you can see different pieces of art, for instance the city's landmark.**

Lehrkraft: That's interesting. Who are the organizers?

Du: **Das klingt interessant. Wer organisiert die Wanderausstellung?**

Mitprüfling: *Eine Künstlergruppe aus Berlin.*

Du: **A group of artists from Berlin.**

Lehrkraft: That's good to know. How much is the entrance fee?

Du: **Und wie viel kostet der Eintritt?**

Mitprüfling: *Der Eintritt für Erwachsene beträgt 6,50 € Ermäßigt beträgt er 4,50 €. Kinder und Jugendliche bis 17 Jahre haben freien Eintritt.*

Du: **Adults must pay € 6.50 and the reduced price is € 4.50. Children and teenagers up to the age of 17 needn't pay any entrance fees.**

Lehrkraft: That's fair. What else should we know?

Du: **Was sollten wir noch wissen?**

Mitprüfling: *In anschließenden Seminaren kann man Enten-Kunstwerke herstellen.*

Du: **There are workshops where you can produce your own duck art pieces.**

Lehrkraft: Oh, I would love to take part. Is it possible to buy souvenirs?

Du: **Daran würde meine Austauschschülerin gerne teilnehmen. Kann man auch Souvenirs kaufen?**

Mitprüfling: *Das ist nur online möglich. Dort sind diverse Fanartikel erhältlich, wie zum Beispiel Bilder, Poster, Postkarten und Bücher.*

Du: **You can only buy souvenirs online. You'll find a variety of fan articles like pictures, posters, postcards and books there.**

Lehrkraft: That sounds great. We will talk to our group and give you a call if we want to come to the exhibition.

Du: **Das klingt toll. Wir werden mit unserer Gruppe sprechen und uns bei Ihnen melden, wenn wir zu der Ausstellung kommen möchten.**

Schriftlicher Teil

LC Listening Comprehension

LC1 A New Trend: Repair Cafés

Hinweis: Bei dieser Aufgabe verfolgst du ein Radiointerview zwischen Megan, der Moderatorin, und dem 16-jährigen Jonathan, der von seiner Tätigkeit in einem Reparaturcafé erzählt. Beachte insbesondere die Fragewörter am Satzanfang und wie viele Antworten gefordert sind („Name one/two"). Wenn du nur eine Antwort lieferst, obwohl zwei gefordert sind, erhältst du dafür 0 Punkte.

0. 16-year-old Jonathan
   Hinweis: Fragewort „who?" → Es wird der Name einer Person gesucht: "Today we say hello to 16-year-old Jonathan" (Z. 1/2)

1. – (skilled) volunteers
   – (local) residents (with broken things)
   Hinweis: Fragewort „who?" → Auch hier geht es um Personen, und zwar darum, welche Personen(gruppen) sich in Reparaturcafés treffen: "A repair café is a meeting place for skilled volunteers and local residents with broken things." (Z. 9/10)

2. (a) protest against the throw-away-culture/repair skills/community spirit
   Hinweis: Fragewort „what?" → Du musst eine Sache aufschreiben, die von Reparaturcafés unterstützt wird. Ein Synonym zum Verb „promote" aus der Frage findest du auch im Hörtext: „support" (Z. 12): "It's a protest against the throw-away-culture. We support repair skills and the community spirit." (Z. 12/13)

3. (in) 2009
   Hinweis: Fragewort „when?" → Es wird eine Zeitangabe benötigt. Lass dich nicht davon irritieren, dass zwei verschiedene Jahreszahlen erwähnt werden; hier wird nach dem allerersten („very first") Reparaturcafé gefragt: "it was first organised by a Dutch journalist in 2009 in the Netherlands." (Z. 15/16)

4. retired persons/unemployed persons/young people (with special talents)/(committed) environmentalists/people interested in repairing things (for free)
   Hinweis: Fragewort „who?" → Wieder musst du zwei Personen(gruppen) nennen, diesmal solche, die in Reparaturcafés mitarbeiten:
   "often they are retired or unemployed persons, but also young people with special talents, they are committed environmentalists and they are interested in repairing things for free." (Z. 19–21)

5. a lot of different things/clothes/electrical devices/(bits of) furniture/bicycles/bikes/mobile phones
   Hinweis: Fragewort „what (kind of)?" → Achte beim Hören darauf, welche Gegenstände erwähnt werden, und nenne zwei davon:
   "Any broken items you can think of – clothes, electrical devices, bits of furniture, bicycles, mobile phones ... – I see, so a lot of different things ..." (Z. 23/24)

6. reducing waste/satisfaction (from repairing things)/fun
   Hinweis: Fragewort „what?" → Die Frage, was Jonathan von seiner Tätigkeit hat, wird im Hörtext etwas anders formuliert: Megan erkundigt sich, warum er dort ohne Bezahlung arbeitet (vgl. Z. 30/31):
   "The philosophy of zero waste, the satisfaction from repairing things [...] and repair cafés are fun and creative." (Z. 32–34)

LC2 My Journey to the Artic Sea

Hinweis: Hier stellt der Wissenschaftler Donald seine Arbeit im Polargebiet vor. Anders als bei der ersten Aufgabe spielt hier die Verwendung der richtigen Grammatik eine Rolle, denn deine Antwort muss den vorgegebenen Satz korrekt vervollständigen. Lies deine Antworten daher am Ende nochmal aufmerksam durch und prüfe, ob der vorgegebene Satzanfang zusammen mit deinem Satzende einen Sinn ergibt. Wenn du einmal mehr als sechs Wörter schreibst, ist das nicht schlimm, versuche dich jedoch kurzzufassen.

0. played outside.
   Hinweis: Ganz am Anfang erzählt Donald von seiner Kindheit in Alaska:
   "We had no TV or computer and so we always played outside with the Inuit children" (Z. 2/3)

1. learn more about the polar regions.
   Hinweis: Achte beim Hören auf das Wort „scientist", das ein Synonym zu „researcher" ist, und was Donald über seine Motivation, ein solcher zu werden, sagt:
   "I knew at a young age I wanted to become a scientist too, to learn more about the polar regions." (Z. 5/6)

2. take pictures (of the animals)/get more people to know about this.
   Hinweis: Achte auf das Signalwort „Antarctica":
   "At some stage I travelled to Antarctica to take pictures of animals." (Z. 7/8), "I just wanted to get more people to know about this and spread this news." (Z. 9/10)

3. (were/are) not touched by it.
   Hinweis: Über die Einstellung vieler Menschen spricht Donald gleich nachdem er erwähnt, dass das Polareis schmilzt:
   "You hear about this quite often on the news, but people were just not touched by that." (Z. 13/14)

4. publish them/touch people's hearts.
   Hinweis: Das Signalwort für diese Aufgabe ist „pictures" (Z. 15):
   "So, I wanted to travel there, take some pictures of the animals and publish them to touch people's hearts." (Z. 14–16)

5. die out (within 50 to 100 years).
   Hinweis: Der Wissenschaft zufolge werden Eisbären aussterben:
   "Scientists predict that polar bears will die out within the next 50 to a 100 years." (Z. 19)

6. (so) skinny/suffering from hunger.
   Hinweis: Höre gut zu, wenn Donald über seine Erfahrungen mit Eisbären berichtet:
   "On my journey I saw a polar bear lying on the shore, hardly any ice around him and he just appeared to be so skinny, and as if he was suffering from hunger." (Z. 20/21)

7. protect this icy wonderland.
   Hinweis: Das Wort "duty" (Z. 29) ist ein Synonym zu „responsiblity" aus der Aufgabenstellung:
   "It is our duty to protect this icy wonderland." (Z. 29)

RC Reading Comprehension

RC1 Vending Machines

Hinweis: Wie der Titel bereits erkennen lässt, stellt dieser Artikel die neuesten Automaten in Singapur und England vor, wobei der Zweck ihrer Verwendung unterschiedlicher kaum sein könnte.
Du musst die Satzanfänge mithilfe von 1–6 Wörtern beenden. Da die Verben, die die gesuchten Informationen im Artikel ankündigen, häufig den einleitenden Verben des vorgegebenen Satzes ähneln, kann es hilfreich sein, die Verben zu vergleichen und nach wiederkehrenden Wörtern bzw. Synonymen zu suchen.

0. luxury vehicles
   Hinweis: "provide" (Aufgabenstellung) → "offering" (Z. 3):
   "A 15-storey building in Singapore is offering luxury vehicles" (Z. 3)

1. a lift-like platform/a moving platform
   Hinweis: "moved by" (Aufgabenstellung) → "brings it down" (Z. 6/7):
   "Once a customer has selected a car to look at, a lift-like platform brings it down to the ground floor." (Z. 6/7)

2. a (modern) snack machine/(modern) snack machines
   Hinweis: Signalwort: "similar to" (Aufgabenstellung) → "The dispensing concept is similar to that of a modern snack machine." (Z. 10/11)

3. (efficient) use of space
   Hinweis: "ensures" (Aufgabenstellung) → "was aimed at" (Z. 17/18):
   "the vending machine format was aimed at making efficient use of space in the city of Singapore where land is scarce." (Z. 17–19)

4. homeless people
   Hinweis: "to support" (Aufgabenstellung) → "to help" (Z. 23):
   "In England the world's first vending machine to help homeless people has recently been installed." (Z. 23/24)

5. support services
   Hinweis: "to show up at" (Aufgabenstellung) → "attend" (Z. 27):
   "To keep the card activated, users must attend support services once a week." (Z. 26/27)

6. (other) support services/charities (in the area)/volunteers/donors/major UK supermarkets
   Hinweis: "gets help" (Aufgabenstellung) → "works with" (Z. 31): "'Action Hunger' works with other support services and charities in the area to provide the free goods they contain. Volunteers keep the machines stocked, and donors include various major UK supermarkets." (Z. 30–33)

RC2 Empowering young People through Snow Sports

Hinweis: Das „Snow-Camp" bringt benachteiligten Jugendlichen das Skifahren näher und kann damit ihr Leben zum Positiven verändern. Nach dem Lesen des Artikels sollst du die Fragen in 1–7 Wörtern oder Zahlen beantworten. Es werden keine Punkte abgezogen, wenn du mehr schreibst. Falls du deine Antworten anders formuliert hast als hier aufgeführt, ist das nicht schlimm; solange der Sinn der gleiche ist, bekommst du dafür auch Punkte.

0. by using their interest in snow sports
   Hinweis: "UK charity Snow-Camp works in deprived inner-city areas to use young people's interest in snow sports" (Z. 1/2)

1. (to) engage them/provide life skills/provide qualifications/provide vocational training
   Hinweis: "to engage them [= young people] and provide life skills, qualifications and vocational training." (Z. 2/3) (zwei dieser Aspekte)

2. (to) serve (an) apprenticeship/(to) become a ski coach/(to)take part in the programme/(to)go on a *(Snow-Camp)* skiing course
   Hinweis: "was offered a year's paid apprenticeship in the snow sports industry." (Z. 7)/"I'm now an internationally-qualified ski coach" (Z. 8)/ "saying 'You know what mum, maybe I am going to go on a Snow-Camp *skiing course'" (Z. 9/10)*

3. he may get involved with gangs/he may gain no GCSEs/he may fail his exams
   Hinweis: "His family were worried he may get involved with gangs and would struggle to gain any GCSEs" (Z. 13–15)

4. (he) wanted to strap on a snowboard/because of *Snow-Camp*
   Hinweis: "was willing to work hard in classroom activities just to be able to strap on a snowboard." (Z. 16/17)/"I did not think that I would enjoy snow sports or want to work hard in a classroom, but with Snow-Camp *I do both" (Z. 18/19)*

5. by becoming a (full-time) snowboard and ski instructor
   Hinweis: "I'm inspired to become a full-time snowboard and ski instructor, showing others the skills that can be learnt through these amazing sports" (Z. 22–24)

6. work with youth projects/work with youth service providers
   *Hinweis: "*Snow-Camp *works directly with youth projects and youth service providers to find participants who are most in need of support." (Z. 26/27)*

7. participants (must) spend as much time on skiing/snowboarding as in the classroom/by providing equal amounts of schooling
   Hinweis: "For every hour the trainees spend learning how to ski or to snowboard, the same amount of time is spent in the classroom." (Z. 30–32)

W Writing Task

School Sports Day

Hinweis: Du bekommst den Auftrag, für die Schulhomepage einen Blogeintrag über den alljährlichen Sporttag, der in der vergangenen Woche stattfand, zu schreiben.
*Zur Vorbereitung solltest du dir Gedanken und Notizen zu den drei Leitfragen machen: An welchen Disziplinen haben du und deine Mitschüler*innen teilgenommen? Was hat dir gut, was weniger gut gefallen und warum? Wie könnte man das Event verbessern?*
Beachte, wie ein Blogeintrag üblicherweise aufgebaut ist: Ein Blogeintrag besteht wie jeder Aufsatz aus einer Einleitung, einem Hauptteil und einem Schluss. Natürlich sollten dein Name und eine einprägsame Überschrift nicht fehlen.

Du richtest dich mit deinem Beitrag an die Schulgemeinschaft. Es ist in Ordnung, auch informelle Sprachelemente zu nutzen. Auch Abkürzungen und direkte Ansprachen sind erlaubt. Dennoch solltest du stets höflich und korrekt bleiben, auch wenn du über Dinge schreibst, die dir am Sporttag nicht gefallen haben.
Natürlich kannst du auch andere Disziplinen und Verbesserungsvorschläge beschreiben als im Lösungsvorschlag. Wichtig ist, dass du alle drei geforderten Aspekte abdeckst. Betrachte das vorgegebene Beispiel als inspirierende Idee und die angegebenen 180 Wörter als Untergrenze.

<u>Annual sports day:</u>
<u>Team spirit, ambition, and power</u>
by Michael Großer (class 10 d)

Überschrift und Name

Dear school community,

Anrede

Under the motto "one class – one team", this year's sports day took place last Tuesday at the sports ground. A week in advance, my classmates and I had enrolled in three different disciplines: ultimate frisbee, sack race and stretching.

Einleitung / *Disziplinen*

Frankly speaking, our 10 d ultimate frisbee team was not as successful as we had expected it to be. Out of six teams we ranked fourth – what a disappointment.

👎

The sack race, on the other hand, was great fun. At the beginning we thought it would not be a problem to beat the pupils of year 5 or 6. But that was a mistake! The younger pupils were very fast. Luckily, my class had the spirit needed and came in second after class 6 b.

👍

The stretching session at the end of that eventful day was a fantastic idea and prevented us from sore muscles the next day. It was also very relaxing after so much effort.

👍

For next year's event, it would be great if everyone could get certificates for taking part and if there were prizes for the three winning classes. *(185 words)*

Verbesserungsvorschlag

Schriftlicher Teil

LC Listening Comprehension

LC1 The Elbphilharmonie

Hinweis: Die Moderatorin Sally heißt Herrn Gerard in ihrer Sendung willkommen. Er beantwortet Sallys Fragen zu Bau, Kosten und verschiedenen Besuchsattraktionen der Hamburger Elbphilharmonie.
Du hörst das Interview zweimal hintereinander. Lass dich durch die Pausen, die nach der Aufgabenvorstellung und vor dem zweiten Durchlauf einsetzen, nicht irritieren. Nutze sie, um dir vor Augen zu führen, welche Informationen du dem Interview entnehmen sollst. Es kann hilfreich sein, Wörter wie „in the end" (Nr. 2), „all attractions" (Nr. 4) und „minimum cost" (Nr. 5) auf dem Aufgabenblatt hervorzuheben.
Es ist nicht nötig, vollständige Sätze zu schreiben, und auch die Zahlen müssen nicht ausgeschrieben werden. Bei dieser Aufgabe reicht es, ca. 1 bis 5 Wörter oder Zahlen zu schreiben.

0. (in) Hamburg's harbour city
   Hinweis: Fragewort „where?" → Es wird nach einem Ort gesucht. „Hamburg" allein reicht als Antwort nicht aus, da nach dem genauen Ort („where exactly") gefragt ist:
   "Well, the Elphi serves as a very important building in Hamburg's Harbour City." (Z. 7/8)

1. (in) 2010
   Hinweis: Fragewort „when?" → Es wird eine Zeitangabe gesucht.
   Auf Sallys Frage, seit wann die Elphi Gäste empfängt, zählt Herr Gerard drei verschiedene Jahreszahlen auf: das Jahr der tatsächlichen Fertigstellung (2016), das ursprünglich geplante Eröffnungsjahr (2010) und das Jahr des Eröffnungskonzertes (2017). Die Frage zielt auf das Jahr ab, in dem das Gebäude eigentlich hätte fertiggestellt werden sollen („supposed to be finished"):
   "The Elphi was finished in November 2016, but the opening was actually planned in 2010." (Z. 12/13)

2. 866 million €

   Hinweis: Fragewort „how much?" → Hier geht es um eine Mengenangabe, und zwar um eine Geldsumme.
   *Auch bei dieser Frage macht Herr Gerard drei verschiedene Angaben. Er benennt die anfänglich kalkulierten Baukosten (77 Millionen €), den tatsächlichen Endpreis (866 Millionen €) und die Steuerkosten für die Hamburger Bürger*innen (200 Millionen €). Gefragt wird aber nur nach den letztendlichen Kosten („in the end"):*
   "The final price then was 866 million €." (Z. 18/19)

3. amazing building/(view from) the viewing balcony/guided tour(s)/concert halls/concerts/hotel

   Hinweis: Fragewort „what?" → Hier musst du zwei Eigenschaften der Elphi aufschreiben, die Gäste anlocken. Diese Informationen sind an verschiedenen Stellen im Text verteilt:
   "amazing building" (Z. 9), "beautiful view from the viewing balcony" (Z. 24), "guided tour that includes the concert halls" (Z. 31/32), "In the Elphi there is a hotel" (Z. 35)

4. 45 € (per person)

   Hinweis: Fragewort „how much?" → Hier geht es um den Preis für ein Ticket, mit dem man alles sehen kann:
   "A guided tour that includes the concert halls costs 45 € per person." (Z. 31/32)

5. 233 €

   Hinweis: Fragewort „what?" → Wieder musst du einen Preis notieren, und zwar den Mindestpreis für eine Hotelübernachtung in der Elphi:
   "In the Elphi there is a hotel [. . .]. The prices for a room are between 233 € and 18,000 €" (Z. 35/36)

LC2 Smart Travelling

Hinweis: Theresa Carey ist zu Gast bei einem Radiosender und stellt den Hörerinnen und Hörern das Couchsurfen vor.
Achte darauf, dass deine Antworten zu den vorgegebenen Satzanfängen passen. Vergisst du beispielsweise das Verb, ergibt der Satz keinen Sinn und du erhältst keinen Punkt, obwohl du den Hörtext eigentlich verstanden hast und die Antwort wusstest. Von daher ist es hier besonders wichtig, nach dem Erfüllen der Aufgabe

deine Antworten erneut zu lesen und zu prüfen, ob sie verständlich und korrekt sind.
Sowohl Bob, der Moderator, als auch Theresa nutzen in ihren Äußerungen häufig hilfreiche Synonyme, die dich zur Lösung führen. In den Hinweisen sind solche Synonyme mit einem Pfeil angegeben.
Beachte auch: Theresa führt oft mehrere Aspekte auf. Du musst allerdings immer nur einen davon nennen.

0. provide a couch or room for free.
   ✎ *Hinweis: „Couchsurfing means" (Aufgabenstellung) → „what couchsurfing is" (Z. 7):*
   "Well, you provide a couch or a room for free." (Z. 8)

1. discovering new places (herself)/travelling on a low budget/offering a couch (to travellers).
   ✎ *Hinweis: „enjoys" (Aufgabenstellung) → „like" (Z. 13)*
   Hier gibt es drei Antwortmöglichkeiten. Bedenke in jedem Fall, dass nach „like" und „enjoy" die -ing-Form folgt:
   "I like discovering new places for myself and travelling on a low budget." (Z. 13/14), "I loved the idea of offering travellers a couch." (Z. 14/15)

2. tell/talk about their (foreign) (life/lives and) culture(s)/leave as friends.
   ✎ *Hinweis: „benefit" (Aufgabenstellung) → „advantages" (Z. 16)*
   Vorteile des Couchsurfens nennt Theresa gleich nachdem sie berichtet, was ihr am Couchsurfen so gut gefällt. Beachte den Unterschied zwischen Frage 1 und 2: Bei 1 geht es um Theresas persönliches Empfinden, bei 2. um allgemeine Vorteile des Couchsurfens:
   "I love hearing about life and cultures in other places. And the people who come often leave as friends." (Z. 17/18)

3. communicate through (the) official channels/review profiles (carefully)/inform friends.
   ✎ *Hinweis: „you can protect yourself" (Aufgabenstellung) → „there is no risk" (Z. 21)*
   Um den „if-clause" zu vervollständigen, musst du deine Antwort mit einem Verb beginnen:
   "There is no risk as long as you communicate through the official channels and review their profiles carefully. Go ahead and inform your friends when a surfer is arriving." (Z. 21–23)

4. look perfect.
   Hinweis: „home" (Aufgabenstellung + Z. 26)
   Die Antwort gibt Theresa, als Bob sie fragt, warum sie kein Geld von ihren Gästen verlangt:
   "I would feel more pressured to have my home look perfect." (Z. 26)

5. rented out her room (to somebody else).
   Hinweis: „first visitor" (Aufgabenstellung) → „first guest" (Z. 29):
   "Do you remember your first guest? – Yes [...] her landlord had rented out her room to somebody else." (Z. 29–31)

6. visited a German father and son/stayed with a young man in Korea/visited Germany and Korea.
   Hinweis: „experienced" (Aufgabenstellung) → „experience" (Z. 37)
   Beachte, dass die richtige Lösung schon vor dem Signalwort „experience" genannt wird:
   "I visited a German father and son, I also stayed with a young man in Korea." (Z. 35/36)

7. have a backup plan/write a review/be open-minded/have fun
   Hinweis: „bear in mind" (Aufgabenstellung) → „advice" (Z. 38)
   Lass dich nicht von der Formulierung „two things" in der Aufgabenstellung verunsichern: Auch hier nennt Theresa mehrere Aspekte, von denen du nur einen aufschreiben musst, denn es heißt explizit „Name one aspect":
   "Always have a backup plan." (Z. 39), "And make sure to write a review afterward." (Z. 40), "Just be open-minded and have fun." (Z. 41)

8. want to be helpful.
   Hinweis: „has taught" (Aufgabenstellung) → „things you've learned" (Z. 42):
   "I've realized that most people really just want to be helpful." (Z. 44)

RC Reading Comprehension

RC1 Smiling – A simple way to be happier

✎ *Hinweis: Eine entscheidende Rolle für das Glücklichsein spielt das Lächeln. Der vorliegende Text geht auf verschiedene Aspekte ein, die mit dem Lächeln in Verbindung stehen. Deine Aufgabe ist es, verschiedene W-Fragen rund um das Thema in ca. 1–6 Wörtern oder Zahlen zu beantworten. Achte auf die Frage- und Signalwörter, die du in den Fragen zum Text findest. Sie weisen dir den Weg zur entsprechenden Stelle im Lesetext und sind in den Hinweisen angegeben, sodass du zunächst dort nachlesen kannst, wenn du dir bei der Lösung unsicher bist.*

0. (the road to) happiness

   ✎ *Hinweis: „globetrotting" (Aufgabenstellung) → „travelling the world" (Z. 1/2):*
   "If you search for the road to happiness, you might start your journey by travelling the world." (Z. 1/2)

1. (in) Thailand

   ✎ *Hinweis: „warm-hearted" (Aufgabenstellung) → „kindness" (Z. 8)*
   Fragewort „where?" → Es wird nach einem Ort gesucht. In dem Artikel werden drei Orte erwähnt, aber nur einer davon wird mit Warmherzigkeit verbunden:
   "[T]he Thai people are frequently displaying bright, full smiles. [...] their smiles come from an <u>inner peace and kindness</u>." (Z. 6–8)

2. 40 to 50 times a day

   ✎ *Hinweis: Fragewort „how often?" → Hier wird eine Häufigkeitsangabe gesucht.*
   „cheerful person" (Aufgabenstellung) → „happy people" (Z. 12):
   "The average person smiles about 20 times a day while <u>happy people smile</u> more often, about <u>40 to 50 times a day</u>." (Z. 12/13)

3. a genuine/real smile

   ✎ *Hinweis: „mood" (Aufgabenstellung) → „emotional state" (Z. 15)*
   Fragewort „what (kind of)?" → Achte auf den Unterschied zwischen „real/genuine smile" und „fake smile", der kurz vor dem Signalwort „emotional state" erklärt wird:

"There seems to be a connection between real happiness and a genuine smile. *A fake smile, however, does not affect your emotional state." (Z. 13–15)*

4. (hundreds of/the) people around you
   Hinweis: „influenced“ (Aufgabenstellung) → „affects“ (Z. 17); Fragewort „who?“ → Die Antwort muss sich auf eine oder mehrere Personen beziehen.
   "A real smile not only affects you but also the people around you." (Z. 17), "the hundreds of people around you can spot your happiness and will most likely be drawn to it." (Z. 20/21)

5. lower blood pressure/fewer stress hormones/(a) longer life
   Hinweis: „health“ (Aufgabenstellung) → „well-being“ (Z. 22) Fragewort „how?“ → Du sollst herausfinden, inwiefern ein Lächeln die Gesundheit fördert. Halte nach einer Auflistung Ausschau und notiere zwei der aufgeführten Aspekte:
   "Scientists agree that a smile can also be quite good for your well-being. Lower blood pressure, fewer stress hormones, a longer life – now that's something to smile about!" (Z. 22–24)

6. quite early/before birth
   Hinweis: „start to smile“(Aufgabenstellung) → „start practising their smile“ (Z. 28)
   Fragewort „when?“ → Es wird nach einem Zeitpunkt gefragt:
   "Humans start practising their smile quite early. In fact, through medical technology, we can see that babies start to smile before birth." (Z. 28/29)

RC2 My life as an online video star

Hinweis: Der Artikel berichtet von der 17-jährigen Allondra Nuñez, einer Vloggerin, und vom 19-jährigen Tyler Sands, der Geld mit Reisevideos verdient. Du musst herausfinden, ob die vorgegebenen Aussagen wahr oder falsch sind, und jeweils den Satz heraussuchen, der deine Entscheidung untermauert. Von diesem Satz musst du als Beleg die ersten vier Wörter herausschreiben.

0. **true**
   justification: **When Mrs Nuñez asked …**
   Hinweis: „assumed“ (Aufgabenstellung) → „expected“ (Z. 1/2):
   “When Mrs Nuñez asked her 17-year-old daughter to search for a job, she expected that Allondra would consider working as a clerk in a grocery store or a shop.” (Z. 1–3)

1. **false**
   justification: **At first, she wasn’t …**
   Hinweis: „Right from the start“ (Aufgabenstellung) → „At first“ (Z. 6):
   “At first, she wasn’t sure what to do in her videos, but then she had the idea to record herself doing what she does best – talking about herself!” (Z. 6–8)

2. **false**
   justification: **It is her warm …**
   Hinweis: „fascinates“ (Aufgabenstellung) → „attracts“ (Z. 9)
   Von Allondras Aussehen ist im Text nicht die Rede. Was ihr Publikum an ihr schätzt, wird im dritten Absatz erklärt:
   “Allondra is positive and genuine; it is her warm personality that attracts thousands of viewers every day to her video blog.” (Z. 9/10)

3. **true**
   justification: **I guess this connected …**
   Hinweis: „relate to“ (Aufgabenstellung) → „connected“ (Z. 16)
   Hier geht es darum, dass das Publikum sich mit Allondra identifizieren kann:
   “I guess this connected with my audience because more than 300,000 fans watched that video.” (Z. 15–17)

4. **false**
   justification: **Mrs Nuñez admits, “I…”/“I wrote in a …”**
   Hinweis: „public“ (Aufgabenstellung) ↔ „confidential“ (Z. 20). Diese Wörter sind Gegensätze. Wenn du das Wort „confidential“ nicht aus dem Kontext erschließen kannst, kannst du es auch im Wörterbuch nachschlagen:
   “Mrs Nuñez admits, ‘I wrote in a diary when I was younger, but I kept it confidential; I hid it under my bed.’” (Z. 19/20)

5. **false**

   justification: **It shocked Tyler Sands' …**

   Hinweis: „profitable business" (Aufgabenstellung) → „able to pay for his entire college tuition" (Z. 25):

   "It shocked Tyler Sands' parents when their 19-year-old son announced that he would be able to pay for his entire college tuition – $ 64,000 for four years." (Z. 24–26)

6. **true**

   justification: **Tyler proudly claims, "I …"/"I have my dream …"**

   Hinweis: „hobby", „profession" (Aufgabenstellung) → „dream job" (Z. 32)

   Tyler betont, dass er seinen Traumjob gefunden hat und dass er dafür bezahlt wird, das zu tun, was ihm Spaß macht. Daraus kannst du schließen, dass er sein Hobby zum Beruf gemacht hat:

   "Tyler proudly claims, 'I have my dream job! I explore cities all over the world and get paid to do it!'" (Z. 31/32)

7. **false**

   justification: **Tyler Sands and Allondra …**

   Hinweis: „footsteps" (Aufgabenstellung) → „never would have thought possible" (Z. 34/35)

   Man erfährt zwar nicht die Berufe der Eltern, aber aus ihren überraschten Reaktionen auf die Berufe ihrer Kinder sowie aus der Tatsache, dass die Eltern den Beruf „Onlinevideostar" vorher gar nicht kannten, geht eindeutig hervor, dass die beiden Jugendlichen nicht in die Fußstapfen ihrer Eltern treten:

   "Tyler Sands and Allondra Nuñez are video stars who are young and are making a lot of money doing something that their parents never would have thought possible." (Z. 33–35)

W Writing Task

Online video channel

Hinweis: Stell dir vor, du möchtest gemeinsam mit deinem englischen Freund bzw. deiner englischen Freundin einen Videochannel starten. Es kann bei der Suche nach Inhalten für die Videos helfen, ein Hobby in deine Überlegungen einzubeziehen. Vielleicht hast du ja sogar englischsprachige Bekannte, mit denen du ein gemeinsames Hobby teilst?
Im Lösungsbeispiel bilden kulturbedingte Unterschiede die Video-Idee. Selbstverständlich gibt es noch viele weitere Möglichkeiten, worüber man hier schreiben kann – deiner Fantasie sind keine Grenzen gesetzt.
Um die volle Punktzahl zu erhalten, ist es wichtig, auf alle Leitfragen einzugehen: Wovon sollen eure Videos handeln? Wie soll euer Channel heißen? Was muss vorab organisiert werden? Wie könnt ihr auf euch aufmerksam machen?
Fasse dich möglichst kurz, dann bleibt dir mehr Zeit, dein Geschriebenes zu überarbeiten und dein Wörterbuch gezielt einzusetzen. Die Mindestanzahl von 180 Wörtern solltest du jedoch erzielen.
Das Lösungsbeispiel fällt mit 256 Wörtern recht lang aus, da es hier und da etwas mehr ins Detail geht, um dir Anregungen zu geben.
Hilfreiche Formulierungen und Übergänge, die deine E-Mail strukturieren, sind unterstrichen. Du kannst sie bei verschiedenen Aufgabenstellungen immer wieder einsetzen.
Da du an eine Person in deinem Alter schreibst, die du gut kennst, darfst du auch Abkürzungen oder informelle Ausdrücke verwenden.

Hello Donna, *Anrede, Begrüßung*

I hope you are alright, and I guess you are as excited as I am regarding our video channel project. During the last couple of days I thought a lot about what we could present to our audience, and I came up with a good idea. Since we often talk about different lifestyles in the UK and in Germany, I think that others might find this interesting, too. Remember for example when we chatted about the recent music charts? *Hinführung zum Thema* *Idee und Begründung*

We could name our channel "Different cultures, different lifestyles". What do you think about that? *Titel*

Before we start our channel, there is still a lot we need to do. As you know, I have a computer and a webcam, but I dislike my headset and would prefer a microphone for our video production. We will also need a good video editing tool. I know you are into video editing, so maybe you can recommend a programme?

Vorbereitungen, Organisation

Moreover, as we want to become successful with our videos, it is necessary to draw attention to our channel. On the one hand we should share our videos on different social networks. On the other hand I suggest that we start following social media stars who publish similar content. We need them to notice and then perhaps follow us back. Then we may even get lucky and perhaps a company may want us to work as influencers. That would be amazing!

Werbung für den Channel

I'm so curious to know whether you like my ideas. Please write back to me soon.

Schluss

Love,
Sandra

Grußformel

(256 words)

Schriftlicher Teil

LC Listening Comprehension

LC1 Australian Bush Fires

Hinweis: Gleich zu Beginn wird dir das Thema des Hörtextes genannt: Ein Reporter erzählt in einem Interview von Waldbränden in Australien. Markiere dir in den 30 Sekunden, in denen du die Aufgabenstellung lesen darfst, wichtige Schlüsselwörter, und achte dann beim Hören auf die gefragten Informationen (z. B. Zeit, Ort, Zahl, Name, etc.). Es reicht, wenn du in Stichpunkten antwortest.

0. September 2019
   Hinweis: Das Schlüsselwort „start" bzw. „started" hilft dir auf die Sprünge.
   "It started from <u>September 2019</u>." (Z. 5)

1. New South Wales/(eastern and north-eastern) Victoria
   Hinweis: Lass dich nicht verunsichern: In der Tabelle steht „two", die Angabe „Name one" sagt dir aber, dass du nur einen der beiden genannten Staaten nennen musst.
   "[T]he fires heavily impacted various regions of the state of <u>New South Wales</u>. In eastern and north-eastern <u>Victoria</u>, large areas of forest burnt" (Z. 5–7)

2. (estimated) 72,000 square miles/mi^2
   Hinweis: „size" → Du musst eine Größenangabe machen.
   "fires this season had burnt an estimated <u>72,000 square miles</u>" (Z. 11/12)

3. two years ago
   Hinweis: „time" → Du musst eine Zeitangabe machen.
   "[T]he <u>last huge fires two years ago</u> burnt about 2,100 premises." (Z. 15/16)

4. (more than) 100 species
   Hinweis: Im relevanten Absatz werden viele Zahlen genannt, achte also darauf, dass du die richtige aufschreibst: Über 100 Arten sind bedroht

(„threatened“), da sie vermutlich bald aussterben:
“More than 100 species are expected to be driven to extinction.” (Z. 22)

5. – (bad) air quality/drop in air quality/air quality dropped
   – (high) expenses/(high) costs (4.4 billion Australian dollars)
   – negative effect on tourism (sector)/less tourism (revenues)
   Hinweis: Nenne zwei der drei im Text erwähnten Folgen.
   “Oh, air quality has dropped to hazardous levels. Expense of dealing with the bushfires is expected to exceed the AU$4.4 billion of the 2009 Black Saturday fires. [. . .] Tourism sector revenues have fallen more than AU$1 billion.” (Z. 25–29)

6. air tanker/(two) helicopter(s)
   Hinweis: Es reicht, wenn du ein Transportmittel nennst.
   “As of 23rd January 2020, an air tanker and two helicopters have crashed during firefighting operations.” (Z. 38/39)

LC2 My year abroad

*Hinweis: Du hörst, wie Richard von seinem High School-Jahr in Spanien und Portugal berichtet. Er bezieht sich hierbei u. a. auf unterschiedliche Essgewohnheiten sowie verschiede Aspekte des Fremdsprachenlernens und die Möglichkeiten moderner Kommunikation, um den Kontakt zu Freund*innen und der Familie aufrecht zu erhalten.*
Bei dieser Aufgabe sind Satzanfänge vorgegeben, die du mit Antworten aus dem Text vervollständigen musst. Es gibt keine maximale Anzahl an Wörtern, die du verwenden darfst, achte aber trotzdem darauf, dich kurzzufassen und nur die geforderte Information aufzuschreiben. Nutze die 30 Sekunden Einlesezeit auch dazu, dir zu überlegen, welche Wortarten in den Sätzen noch benötigt werden. Ist z. B. bereits ein vollständiges Prädikat enthalten oder benötigst du dieses noch, um den Satz sinnvoll zu vervollständigen?

0. share his experience.
   Hinweis: „now“ (Aufgabenstellung) → „recently“ (Z. 1)
   “I want to share my experience” (Z. 2)

1. moved to Lisbon/Portugal.
   Hinweis: „After“ (Aufgabenstellung + Z. 4)
   “After one semester, I moved from Barcelona to Lisbon.” (Z. 4/5)

2. couldn't get any better.
   Hinweis: „didn't want to" (Aufgabenstellung) → „didn't like the idea" (Z. 6)
   "I assumed it couldn't get any better than Barcelona" (Z. 6/7)

3. discover (exciting) new food.
   Hinweis: „Being sick of English meals" (Aufgabenstellung) → „tired of fish and chips and English breakfast" (Z. 12);
   „glad to" (Aufgabenstellung) → „very happy to" (Z. 12/13)
   "I was tired of fish and chips and English breakfast and very happy to discover exciting new food." (Z. 12/13)

4. keep up with two/three languages.
   Hinweis: „forget words" (Aufgabenstellung) → „forget English terms" (Z. 18);
   „hard" (Aufgabenstellung) → „very difficult" (Z. 19)
   "It turned out to be very difficult to keep up with two – or in my case even three – languages." (Z. 19/20)

5. gaining knowledge of a (foreign) culture.
   Hinweis: „leads to" (Aufgabenstellung) → „contributes to " (Z. 23);
   Höre gut hin, wenn das Schlüsselwort „slang" zum ersten Mal genannt wird (vgl. Z. 22).
   "[S]lang contributes to gaining knowledge of a foreign culture." (Z. 23/24)

6. create a bit of home/have video calls/share (your) adventures.
   Hinweis: „[t]echnical devices" (Aufgabenstellung) → „modern technology" (Z. 26)
   "thanks to modern technology, even abroad you can create a bit of home. It's easy to have a video call with your friends and family and share your adventures." (Z. 25–27)

7. (has) taught him a lot/taught him so much/was an adventure.
   Hinweis: „[i]n conclusion" (Aufgabenstellung) → „all in all" (Z. 27/28);
   „high school year" (Aufgabenstellung) → „year abroad" (Z. 28)
   "So all in all, my year abroad has taught me so much [. . .] It's not only an adventure, it's also about growing as a person." (Z. 27–29)

RC Reading Comprehension

RC1 You're never too old for amusement parks

Hinweis: Die Erzählerin berichtet von ihrer Leidenschaft für Freizeitparks. Insbesondere geht sie auf den Park „Amazing Land of Adventure" ein und beschreibt dessen besonderen Aufbau sowie seine Attraktionen.
Lies den Text sorgfältig und entscheide dann, ob die Aussagen richtig oder falsch sind. Zusätzlich sollst du jeweils eine Zeilenangabe aus dem Text hinzufügen, die deine Antwort begründet. Wenn du nicht sicher bist, markiere Schlüsselwörter in der Aussage und suche mit ihrer Hilfe die entsprechenden Stellen im Text.

0. **true** (ll. 2/3)
   Hinweis: „little kid" (Aufgabenstellung) → „six years old" (Z. 3)
   "I visited my first amusement park when I was six years old and I have loved them ever since." (Z. 2/3)

1. **false** (ll. 6/7)
   Hinweis: „daily life" (Aufgabenstellung) → „everyday life " (Z. 7)
   "I leave the dull everyday life behind" (Z. 6/7)

2. **true** (ll. 11–13)
   Hinweis: „ears, eyes, hands and more" (Aufgabenstellung) → „senses: sight, sound, touch, taste, and smell" (Z. 12/13)
   "The park is arranged into five different areas – one for each of the senses: sight, sound, touch, taste, and smell." (Z. 11–13)

3. **false** (l. 16)
   Hinweis: Das Schlüsselwort „labyrinth" kommt in der Aufgabenstellung und in Z. 15 vor, das zweite Schlüsselwort „special" in der Aufgabenstellung und in Z. 16.
   "a labyrinth [. . .] where you have to wear special dark glasses so that you can't see." (Z. 15/16)

4. **true** (ll. 20/21)
   Hinweis: „jungle" (Aufgabenstellung) → „rainforest" (Z. 21)
   "you hear birds, insects, and other animals. It is like you are in the rainforest." (Z. 20/21)

5. **false** (ll. 23–27)
   Hinweis: „around the world" (Aufgabenstellung) → „in other countries" (Z. 24)
   Achtung: Hier ist der erste Teil der Aussage richtig (man kann Leute aus der ganzen Welt treffen), der zweite aber falsch (man spielt keine Offline-, sondern Onlinespiele). Die Gesamtaussage ist demnach falsch.
   "Here you can connect digitally with other kids in other countries. [...] even played an online video game with a kid in Ghana." (Z. 23–27)

6. **true** (ll. 31/32)
   Hinweis: „too old" (Aufgabenstellung) → „too mature" (Z. 31); „reconsider" (Aufgabenstellung) → „think again" (Z. 31)
   "If you think you are too mature for amusement parks, think again. You are never too old to have fun!" (Z. 31/32)

RC2 The new shopping experience

Hinweis: In diesem Text wird eine neue Art des automatischen Einkaufens mithilfe einer App und eines Scanners am Einkaufskorb beschrieben. Lies die Beschreibung eines solchen Einkaufs aufmerksam und kreuze anschließend jeweils zu den vorgegebenen Satzanfängen das richtige Satzende an.

0. **b** shoplifting goods.
   Hinweis: „seems to be" (Aufgabenstellung) → „assuming" (Z. 3); „shoplifting" (Antwort b) → „stolen" (Z. 3);
   "You may be assuming that this woman has just stolen from the store." (Z. 3)

1. **c** look into security devices.
   Hinweis: „identify" (Aufgabenstellung)) → „identified" (Z. 11); „look into" (Antwort c) → „glances up" (Z. 5)
   Antwort b scheint auf den ersten Blick auch plausibel, ist aber falsch, da es nicht nur um die Augen geht, sondern um das ganze Gesicht, das von den Kameras erkannt wird.
   "As she enters the store, she removes her sunglasses and glances up at the 12 cameras over the door." (Z. 5/6); "She was identified by facial recognition cameras as she entered the store." (Z. 11)

2. **c** put them in her backpack.
   Hinweis: „backpack" (Antwort c) → „rucksack" (Z. 9)
   "Once she has finished, she transfers the items from the basket to her rucksack and leaves the store." (Z. 8/9)

3. **b** finding the location of the desired items.
   Hinweis: „finding the location" (Antwort b) → „where to go" (Z. 16/17)
   "If she had needed assistance finding something then the app on her phone would have directed her where to go." (Z. 15–17)

4. **a** reconsider a former choice.
   Hinweis: „reconsider" (Antwort a) → „changes her mind" (Z. 17)
   "The 'smart' basket can even recognize if she changes her mind about an item." (Z. 17/18)

5. **c** offer automated shopping.
   Hinweis: „Some companies" (Aufgabenstellung) → „Some stores" (Z. 20)
   Lass dich nicht von Antwort a verunsichern: Sie ist fasch, da „forbid" genau das Gegenteil des Wortes „allow" aus dem Text (vgl. Z. 21)ist.
   "Some stores in big cities have begun allowing this kind of individual shopping where everything is done through automation" (Z. 20–22)

6. **a** minimize social contacts.
   Hinweis: Die Antwort auf diese Frage findest du an verschiedenen Stellen zwischen den Zeilen:
   "nothing requires person-to-person contact" (Z. 22); "Automated shopping makes it easy to avoid people who may be sick. (Z. 25/26)

7. **b** offering better alternatives.
   Hinweis: „alternatives" (Antwort a) → „choices" (Z. 28), „options" (Z. 30)
   "The app can even make recommendations for what foods might be healthier options for the next time you shop." (Z. 29–31)

W Writing Task

Robots in schools

Hinweis: Du sollst einer gleichaltrigen englischsprachigen Person eine E-Mail zu der Frage schreiben, ob Roboter Lehrkräfte an Schulen ersetzen sollten.
Gehe auf alle Bereichen der Aufgabenstellung ein: auf die technische Ausstattung, die an deiner Schule verwendet wird, darauf, was Roboter im Vergleich zu Lehrkräften (nicht) können und auf die Frage, ob Roboter Lehrkräfte ersetzen sollten.
Es ist ebenfalls wichtig, eine informelle Anrede sowie eine Grußformel für den Schluss zu verwenden und deinen Text logisch und gut gegliedert aufzubauen.
Im Hinblick auf die sprachlichen Anforderungen erhältst du unter anderem Punkte, wenn du deine Sätze mit Konnektoren verknüpfst. Es bietet sich zum Beispiel an, deine Argumente mit „on the one hand … on the other hand", „additionally" oder „in the first place" zu verbinden bzw. mit „because" zu begründen. Solche nützlichen Wendungen sind in der Beispiellösung unterstrichen, damit du sie dir gut merken kannst.
Die folgende Beispiellösung soll dir einige Ideen zur Umsetzung der Aufgabe geben, deshalb ist sie etwas länger als die geforderten 180 Wörter. Wenn du andere Argumente gesammelt hast, ist das natürlich nicht falsch, sofern du sie sinnvoll begründest und logisch einbaust.

Dear Tom, *Anrede, Begrüßung*

Einleitung

How are you? I recently read an article about robots in schools and had to think about you because of your interest in technology. The writer asked whether robots should replace teachers and I would like to share my thoughts about it with you.

Technologien an der eigenen Schule

At my school the pandemic has changed the use of technology. In addition to a projector, there is now also a computer and a document scanner in every classroom. Moreover, we can use a newly set up Wi-Fi in the whole building and students from the graduating classes work with tablets which are provided by the school. These devices make learning much easier because you can save notes faster and look at pictures and watch videos to support your learning process.

But I think that if teachers were replaced by modern technology like robots there would be a lot of disadvantages.
Of course on the one hand, robots can be programmed with a huge amount of knowledge and can answer almost every question. Furthermore, they are never tired in the morning and if they are damaged you can just fix them with the right tool or replace them with a newer model.
But on the other hand, robots cannot be emotional or react to a student's personal problems, and neither do they have social or creative skills. Moreover, if you ask a robot a question in the wrong way or if you do not pronounce words clearly you might get a completely wrong answer or reaction.
To sum up, I prefer human teachers. What is your opinion?

Best wishes,
Emma *(266 words)*

Überleitung zur Frage „Sollen Roboter Lehrkräfte ersetzen?" Fähigkeiten und Vorteile von Robotern

Nachteile von Robotern

Schluss: Beantwortung der Frage
Grußformel: Verabschiedung

Sprachpraktische Prüfung

Hinweis: In der sprachpraktischen Prüfung kommt es auf viele verschiedene Faktoren an. Es geht nicht ausschließlich darum, jede Vokabel einwandfrei zu beherrschen, sondern es wird zum Beispiel auch bewertet, wie du englische Wörter, die dir gerade nicht einfallen, erklärst und wie fließend du sprichst.

Monologue

Hinweis: Der Monolog ist in drei Aufgabenstellungen untergliedert. Lies dir zu Beginn alle drei Aufgaben durch, damit du möglicherweise bereits geeignete Übergänge formulieren kannst.
In Kapitel 4.3 des Trainingsbands findest du hilfreiche Formulierungen für die einzelnen Prüfungsabschnitte. Solche Wendungen, die immer wieder passen, sind in den folgenden Lösungsvorschlägen unterstrichen.

Different Lifestyles

1. *Hinweis: Im Idealfall beziehst du dich bei der Beschreibung der beiden Bilder bereits auf auffällige Unterschiede, die du gut für die zweite Aufgabe nutzen kannst, wie z. B. die Orte, an denen die Bilder entstanden sind, oder die dargestellten Personen.*

   In the first picture, you can see a woman with a dog from behind. They're looking at a mountain in front of them. There are several mountains which you can see in the background of the picture. The woman is wearing hiking clothes and a backpack. She seems to enjoy being outside in nature. There's nobody else around, so I think it must be very quiet.
   In the second picture, there's a businessman sitting at his desk. He's wearing a suit and is probably very busy with work because he's doing several things at the same time: typing on his laptop, looking at a paper and taking something from his desk. On the left side of the desk there are a lamp and a laptop, also you can see some pens, paper and a tablet in the middle of the desk. Behind the man there's a cupboard with books.

2. *Hinweis: Für die zweite Aufgabe sollst du die beiden in den Bildern dargestellten Lebensstile miteinander vergleichen. Dies hast du ggf. bereits in der ersten Aufgabe durch verschiedene Adjektive wie „quiet" und „busy" eingeleitet. Du kannst auch auf die mit den Lebensstilen verbundenen Gefühle eingehen.*

   The lifestyles shown in the pictures are very different. I think the first picture represents a very relaxed lifestyle. People living such a lifestyle probably need peace and quiet to regenerate, love to be surrounded by nature and don't need a lot of money to be happy. Perhaps the woman in the picture prefers having time for herself and with her dog instead of being in a big city with many people.
   The second picture shows the opposite. I suppose the man loves being successful in his job, working long hours, earning a lot of money and living a luxurious life. For me this rather represents the lifestyle of big, hectic cities than the one of peaceful nature. I would also assume that what others think about him and what he has achieved in life is very important for the man.

3. *Hinweis: Beschreibe verschiedene Entwürfe für ein glückliches Leben und stelle sie gegenüber. Wichtig ist, dass du deine Erläuterungen gut begründest, beispielsweise, indem du dich in Menschen hineinversetzt, die ein solches Leben führen. Was könnte sie daran glücklich machen? Die Bilder geben dir bereits zwei Ideen, aber natürlich kannst du auch weitere Ideen ergänzen. Möglicherweise hast du selbst schon eine Vorstellung von deinem zukünftigen Leben und kannst sie miteinbeziehen.*

   Firstly, happiness in life can be achieved by spending a lot of time with people you love. Those people can be very good friends or your family. If this is what makes you happy, it's likely that you'll start a family of your own. Supporting and caring for each other, sharing love and making the same memories can connect you with others and therefore fulfill you.
   Another concept of a happy life can be being by yourself and living a slow and quiet life. People choosing this life concept often get their energy from being in nature, meditating or practising yoga, for example. I suggest this is the life the woman in picture one prefers.
   Lastly, I would like to talk about the life concept of the businessman in picture two. For him, wealth and possession might be the things that make him most happy. If this is true for you, you probably focus on your job and becoming successful and earning a lot of money is what drives you.

Personally, I'd prefer the first option. If I just focused on a career, I'd become lonely and rather sad. The same could happen if I spent too much time being on my own.

Upcycling

1. ✎ *Hinweis: Achte besonders auf die dargestellten Gegenstände und deren Verwendung beziehungsweise Umgestaltung. Im zweiten Bild solltest du auch die dargestellte Person, insbesondere ihren Gesichtsausdruck, beschreiben und Vermutungen über ihre Gefühle äußern.*

   In the centre of the first picture, there are two footballs of which parts have been cut out and which are being used as plant pots. They are surrounded by other potted plants and flowers, so I think that this picture shows the terrace in someone's garden.
   The second picture shows a woman standing behind a chair. In her left hand she's holding a brush and in her right hand you can see a small pot of paint. The background of the picture looks like a garage or a workshop because there are saws hanging on a wall. The woman must love what she's doing there because she looks happy and is smiling at the camera. This is possibly her workplace where she upcycles different furniture.

2. ✎ *Hinweis: Nenne verschiedene Gegenstände und erkläre, wie sie mit etwas Kreativität in etwas Neues verwandelt werden können. Denke beispielsweise an Projekte deines Kunstunterrichts oder gehe in Gedanken durch dein Zimmer und überlege, welche Dinge dort upgecycelt werden könnten.*

   My first idea of things that can be modified easily are clothes. For example, it's very easy to change jeans into summer shorts or long-sleeved shirts into T-shirts if you just cut off pieces. Also, you can use other material like old bedding or curtains to create something completely new like a dress or even a costume for the next party.
   What also comes to my mind are euro-pallets used to create furniture. A lot of people have sofas on their balconies and terraces which are made from euro-pallets. But that's not the only thing you can use them for. I once slept in a hotel room with only euro-pallet-made furniture!
   Finally, I'd like to mention glass containers of any shape and kind, such as jars from the supermarket or empty bottles. You can use them to put flowers and plants inside, for the pens on your desk or as a candleholder. With

pearls, paper or other material every glass container can get its own individual design, too.

3. *Hinweis: Du sollst erklären, warum es wichtig ist, Dingen ein zweites Leben zu geben. Diese Fragestellung zielt auf das Thema Nachhaltigkeit ab und auf die Folgen für unsere Umwelt, wenn wir Dinge entsorgen anstatt sie zu recyceln oder weiterzugeben.*

   In my opinion, there are several reasons why it's important to reuse objects. I'll point out the most important ones.
   To start with, a lot of items like electronic devices or clothes that are thrown away aren't broken or useless. Of course, if there's damage, you can also try to repair them. Often other people who can't afford new things are happy to get your old things.
   Furthermore, the old owner can earn some money too by selling belongings instead of putting them into the bin.
   However, the most important reason for reusing objects is the future of our planet. Reusing items and trying to save our planet have recently become even more common topics. Some of the problems we're facing are the huge amount of plastic trash in the oceans as well as the increasing pollution. Throwing away things we don't want any more increases these issues. Reusing objects instead of buying new ones saves a lot of energy and resources.

Plastic

1. *Hinweis: Beschreibe bei diesen beiden Bildern, die sich im ersten Moment sehr ähnlich zu sein scheinen, möglichst genau die Unterschiede, die du erkennst. Achte zum Beispiel darauf, wo sich die beiden Szenen abspielen.*

   Both of the pictures show places where fruit and vegetables are sold. There's a big choice of different kinds of fresh food in the first and in the second picture.
   I think the first picture was taken at a street market because the fruit and vegetables are placed in boxes with hand-written price tags on cardboard inside each box and because the food isn't packed. A man, apparently a customer, is looking at the food.
   In comparison, the second picture seems to show a typical supermarket because there are shelves with perfectly sorted fruit and vegetables and

printed price tags placed below. Additionally, everything is packed or wrapped up in plastic. Also, there's a woman who's picking something and using a trolley for her shopping.

2. *Hinweis: Auch wenn die Bilder ausschließlich Lebensmittel zeigen, umfasst diese Fragestellung natürlich alle Verpackungen aus Plastik und beispielsweise auch Plastik-Einkaufstüten Du kannst also auch über andere Produkte sprechen, die in Plastik verpackt sind, zum Beispiel Kleidung. Begründe deine Haltung.*

   From my point of view, most plastic used for fresh food in supermarkets is useless. I can't understand why cucumbers or broccoli are individually wrapped in plastic. When I'm shopping with my parents, we try to buy things without plastic packaging and avoid taking those small plastic bags offered when we buy more than one apple, for example.
   Moreover, we always bring our own shopping bags or a big box to carry our shopping home with us and thus avoid buying new plastic bags all the time. Particularly after having learned at school about what happens to all the plastic that people throw away, I'm trying to be even more careful about not contributing to plastic waste.

3. *Hinweis: In dieser Aufgabe sollst du am Beispiel deines Lieblingsjoghurts aufzeigen, wie man mit Plastikverpackungen umgehen kann. Es wird erwartet, dass du dich am Ende für eine der Alternativen entscheidest. Vergiss nicht, deine Entscheidung gut zu begründen.*

   In my opinion, there are three options. First, I can just not think about the consequences and keep on buying my favourite yoghurt in a plastic cup. But certainly this would be the worst alternative, so I'll mention two more.
   The second possibility is to find another yoghurt with a similar taste that comes in a glass jar or without packaging – today there are more and more shops which sell all their items without any packaging and customers can bring their own containers.
   The last option is also the one that requires the most effort. I could try getting in contact with the company that produces my yoghurt, explain to them why I wish them to change their packaging and maybe also encourage others to do the same.
   All in all, I'd probably choose the second alternative because there are many different yoghurts on the market and I'm sure to find another one I like.

Dialogue

✎ Hinweis: Achtet darauf, alle vorgegebenen Ideen miteinzubeziehen. Sie helfen euch dabei, die erwarteten sechs Gesprächsminuten zu erreichen und eine Einigung zu erzielen. Es geht nicht darum, den Mitprüfling zu überbieten, sondern darum, zusammenzuarbeiten und eine gemeinsame Auswahl zu treffen.
Wie beim Monolog sind hilfreiche Formulierungen, die immer wieder passen, in den folgenden Lösungsvorschlägen unterstrichen.

Opening Ceremony

Candidate A: Hi Laura! How are you?

Candidate B: Hey Alex! I'm already excited about the opening of our new school buildings next year. How about you?

Candidate A: Oh, I'm excited, too. Let's collect some ideas for the opening. What should we plan to make the ceremony a success for everyone?

Candidate B: In my opinion, we definitely need good music. We could invite bands from different schools. What do you think about that?

Candidate A: I agree on having live music in general, but why should we invite bands from other schools? We have several bands at our school who can play. I'm worried it'll turn out into a competition of schools.

Candidate B: Oh, that's a good argument. We have three school bands, that'll be enough. But I've just had another idea when you were talking about competitions. We can organize a football match between students and teachers. That'd be fun, won't it?

Candidate A: Hmm, wouldn't that take up too much time?

Candidate B: You're probably right. What else do you suggest?

Candidate A: I've heard that the drama club is planning their new play soon. We could also ask them if they want to have their premiere at the opening? There'll be a big audience.

Candidate B: Well, nice plan, but that would take up a lot of time, too. And what if it's too busy at the ceremony? People probably won't be focused on a theatre play.

Candidate A: You've got a point there. The drama club should have their audience's full attention for a premiere.

Candidate A: But we need something official. Something like a speech given by the principal, for example.

Candidate B: Absolutely! I think our principal should open the ceremony and after the speech the bands can start playing.

Candidate A: Perfect! But we haven't talked about drinks and snacks so far. How about organizing an international buffet?

Candidate A: I really like that idea! We have so many international students here. It'll be great to represent every nation with our buffet. We can ask students and parents to prepare something for the buffet.

Candidate B: That sounds like a plan. I'm already getting hungry!

Candidate A: Lastly, how about guided tours inside the new buildings?

Candidate B: Hmm, the parents will also be there and I don't think tours would be very interesting for them, would they?

Candidate A: Okay, that's true, so no guided tours.

Candidate B: I guess we have a plan now: our school bands, a speech by the principal and an international buffet. Let's meet after the break tomorrow and present our ideas to the principal.

Candidate A: Great plan! I'm sure she'll like them! See you tomorrow, Alex!

Candidate B: Bye, Laura!

How to spend money

Candidate A: Hey Toby! How was your weekend?

Candidate B: Hello Lisa! It was great. How are you?

Candidate A: I'm fine. Thank you.

Candidate B: So crazy how time flies. It's the end of the school year already. So let's talk about some ideas of how to spend the rest of our class money. Have you got any suggestions?

Candidate A: I thought about planning a movie night. We could use the money to buy a film and to order some snacks. What do you say?

Candidate B: Well, how to decide on the right movie? I guess there are a lot of different tastes and it might be difficult to find something everybody likes. Have you considered that?

Candidate A: You're right, but we can do a survey or let everyone vote for their favourite choice. If we start early, we'll also be able to watch two films of two different genres.

Candidate B: Sounds good, but either way I'd prefer something where no compromises would have to be made. I really like the part with the food. So what's your opinion on a dinner with our teachers? We could form groups and each group prepares something for a buffet. We can ask if we can use our school kitchen and the dining room.

Candidate A: On the one hand, I really like this idea, but on the other hand, it'll be a lot of work. We need to go shopping for the ingredients in advance, plan that people don't bring in the same thing and so on. Maybe we should also think about something you can keep as a memory. For example, we can create graduation T-shirts with all our names on them. Additionally, we can do a professional photo shoot with all of us wearing the T-shirts. That'll be nice to remember our school time in ten or twenty years.

Candidate B: Oh, what a cool idea! So far, this is my number one, really! But do we have any more ideas?

Candidate A: Yes, we should also consider taking the money for a farewell class trip. For example, we could spend two nights in a hostel which isn't too far away and go there by train. In the evenings we could watch movies or presentations of old class photos. I think this will be cool!

Candidate B: Oh, definitely! But we don't have enough money left for two nights in a hostel and train tickets for everyone, I'm afraid. Everybody would have to pay additional money for it. I'm not sure if this is possible.

Candidate A: True. We were asked to spend the leftovers, not to collect more money.

Candidate B: There's one more idea I have. I've heard about a lot of charity events recently. We could also join one of them and donate our money for a good cause.

Candidate A: Oh, you're too good! But we should decide on an idea for the class. After comparing all of what we've talked about, I really am for the T-shirts and the photo shoot. We can either do the shoot before and use the photo for the shirts or take photos with us wearing the T-shirts. And why not donate the rest of the money to a charity?

Candidate B: That's a good idea. I'll phone some printing companies and photographers later to collect prices.

Candidate A: Oh, thank you for doing that. Then we'll see how much is left for the charity and we can present our ideas to our classmates.

Candidate B: Sure! Have a good afternoon and see you tomorrow in class!

Tablets in Class

Candidate A: Hello Peter!

Candidate B: Hi Mara, nice to see you!

Candidate A: Nice to see you, too. How cool that we'll get tablets for our school, don't you think?

Candidate B: Well, of course tablets offer a lot of opportunities, but there are also some negative aspects to consider. For example, we don't have a very stable Wi-Fi connection at school, so that might make it difficult for us to use the tablets properly.

Candidate A: I see, but the technical support will fix that soon. The Wi-Fi has just been set up and maybe it's just a matter of time till they sort out all the problems.

Candidate B: Okay, I agree, but what about our data? There must be a secure network to make sure nothing falls into wrong hands.

Candidate A: Of course it's important to double check, but I'm sure the school would only use safe connections and maybe also two-step verification.

Candidate B: Yes, you're right. I just get a bit worried sometimes. Do you know how the costs for the tablets are covered? Will there be a sponsor?

Candidate A: The principal told me that there's a department from the government which will pay for them. But there's not enough money to buy a tablet for each student, so only the class 5 and 6 pupils will get some at first.

Candidate B: Okay, and which model will they get?

Candidate A: I hope they'll buy iPads, they're the best.

Candidate B: iPads are the most expensive models on the market. If we buy cheaper models, we'll be able to buy more and therefore more students will be able to go digital.

Candidate A: That's a good argument. I agree. Do you know which brand has the best price for what it offers?

Candidate B: Not now, but I'll do some research for when we have to present our ideas.

Candidate A: Good, thank you. Let's talk about the subjects in which it's useful to work with tablets. I think we can use them perfectly for maths and science. There are good programmes for solving difficult tasks.

Candidate B: That's right! But tablets can be used in every subject. There are also apps for the revision of vocabulary, for creating art projects like films or for editing photos and we could write our essays on it.

Candidate A: Brilliant! I hadn't considered all those aspects. But what about the students and teachers who don't know how to use tablets appropriately?

Candidate B: I'm sure there aren't too many students who don't know how to work with a tablet, but some companies offer free training sessions. We could ask the principal to arrange that if anybody's interested.

Candidate A: That's a good idea. So we both recommend buying tablets, don't we?

Candidate B: Yes, absolutely. Particularly after our experience during the pandemic and because everything really is being digitalised, it's really important that we establish new media in our schools.

Candidate A: True! So see you tomorrow!

Candidate B: See you! Bye!

Mediation

Hinweis: Deine Lehrkraft übernimmt die Position der englischsprachigen Person und stellt dir Fragen, die du auf Deutsch an deinen Mitprüfling weitergibst. Er/sie liest die deutschen Antworten vor, die du wiederum auf Englisch an deine Lehrkraft weitergibst. In der Prüfung findet die Mediation komplett mündlich statt, du hast also die Informationen nicht schriftlich vor dir wie beim Üben mit diesem Buch.

Es kommt nicht darauf an, wörtlich zu übersetzen, sondern inhaltlich korrekt wiederzugeben, was gesagt wurde. Wenn du eine Vokabel nicht weißt, umschreibe sie oder nutze Synonyme.

Es kann vorkommen, dass dein Mitprüfling oder deine Lehrkraft bei einer bestimmten Frage sehr viele Informationen für dich haben und du dir nicht alles auf einmal merken kannst. In diesem Fall kannst du einfach nachfragen und um eine Wiederholung bitten (ohne Punktabzug). Achte darauf, dass du bei der jeweils richtigen Sprache bleibst und deine Rolle in der gegebenen Situation beibehältst.

Alpaka Spaziergang

Lehrkraft (= Engländer*in): Excuse me, we'd like to know something about the animals. Why are they here?

Du: Entschuldigen Sie. Diese Familie möchte/würde gerne etwas über die Tiere erfahren. Warum sind sie hier?

Mitprüfling (= Mitarbeiter/in Infostand): *Wir machen hier Werbung für einen Bauernhof, der Erlebnisse mit Alpakas anbietet.*

Du: They're advertising a farm which offers activities with alpacas.

✎ *Hinweis: Wenn dir z.B. die Übersetzung von „Alpakas" nicht einfällt, umschreibe das Tier, z.B. so:* "a hairy animal/An animal that (mostly) lives in Peru/South America and belongs to the family of camels/looks a bit like a camel"

Lehrkraft: That sounds interesting. But why alpacas? And what kind of activities?

Du: (Aber) warum Alpakas? Und welche Art von Aktivitäten?

Mitprüfling: *Alpakas können dabei helfen, Ruhe im stressigen Alltag zu finden. Man macht einen Spaziergang mit den Tieren und verbringt Zeit auf der Weide mit ihnen.*

Du: Alpacas can help people to relax/to find peace/to find quiet on a stressful day. You take a walk/go for a walk with the animals and spend some time with them on grazing land.

✎ *Hinweis: Eine Umschreibung für „Weide" kann z.B. sein:* "something like a field with grass/where farm animals like cows, sheep or alpacas spend the day and eat"

Lehrkraft: Okay, I get the idea of walking with the alpacas. But how do you relax by just spending time with them?

Du: Sie verstehen, warum man mit den Alpakas spazieren gehen sollte. Aber wie kann man sich entspannen, wenn man (einfach) nur mit den Tieren Zeit verbringt/zusammen ist?

Mitprüfling: *Man verhält sich ruhig und beobachtet die Alpakas. Die Tiere nähern sich bei Stille und ihre Gelassenheit überträgt sich auf den Menschen.*

Du: You stay quiet/relaxed and just watch the alpacas. The animals come closer when there's silence and their serenity passes on/is transferred to the people.

✎ *Hinweis: Da Wort „Gelassenheit" kannst du z.B. folgendermaßen umschreiben:* peace of mind, patience, calmness; unstressed character

Lehrkraft: Hmm, that's really hard to imagine but maybe we should give it a try. How much is it?

Du: Sie fragen, was der Ausflug kostet.

Mitprüfling: *Der Spaziergang von etwa 2 Stunden kostet 28 €. Der Aufenthalt auf der Weide von ebenfalls etwa 2 Stunden kostet 15 €.*

Du: **A walk of around 2 hours costs €28. Staying/Being with them on the grazing land for around 2 hours costs €15.**

✎ *Hinweis: Achte auf Währungen. Da man ins Englische übersetzt, vergisst man gerade in der Prüfungssituation leicht, dass die Preise in Euro statt Dollar oder Pfund genannt werden.*

Lehrkraft: That sounds fair. Is it also possible to stay on the farm overnight?

Du: **Sie fragen, ob es auch möglich ist, auf dem Bauernhof zu übernachten/ob man auch auf dem Bauernhof übernachten kann.**

Mitprüfling: *Ja, man kann dort in Zimmern oder Ferienwohnungen übernachten. Die Preise variieren je nach Größe. Nähere Infos dazu gibt es auf der Homepage.*

Du: **Yes, you can stay there in rooms or apartments. Prices vary according to/depend on the size of the room. You can get more information on their homepage.**

✎ *Hinweis: Wenn du dir bei dem Abschnitt „variieren je nach" unsicher bist, kannst du auch einen „if-clause" daraus machen:* "It's cheaper if you have a small room and more expensive if you book a bigger room."

Lehrkraft: I'm sure the kids would love to spend time on the alpaca farm. Is there anything else we should know?

Du: **Gibt es noch etwas, dass die Familie wissen sollte?**

Mitprüfling: *Eine Reservierung im Voraus ist nötig, da es in den Ferien und an den Wochenenden hohe Besucherzahlen gibt.*

Du: **It's required that you/You must book in advance because particularly at the weekends and in the holidays there are a lot of visitors.**

✎ *Hinweis: Wenn du dir bei der Übersetzung von „Reservierung" unsicher bist, denke zuerst an deutsche Synonyme, dann wird dir schnell das Wort „Buchung" einfallen, das du mit* booking *(Verb: „to book") übersetzen kannst. Für „im Voraus" kannst du alternativ auch* before *benutzen:* "You must book a room before you can stay there."

Lehrkraft: We'll definitely do that. Thank you very much for your help.

Du: **Sie werden das auf jeden Fall machen und bedanken sich für Ihre Hilfe.**

Repair Café

Lehrkraft (= Engländer): Excuse me, I'd like to know more about this repair café? What exactly is it?

Du: Entschuldigen Sie, unser Austauschschüler würde gerne mehr über das Repair Café wissen. Was genau ist das?

Mitprüfling (= AG-Leiter): *Es ist keine normale Werkstatt, sondern Hilfe zur Selbsthilfe. Man kann die Wartezeit mit Kaffee und Kuchen überbrücken.*

Du: It's no ordinary workshop, but/rather a place that helps people to help themselves. You can have coffee and cake there while you wait.

✎ *Hinweis: „Hilfe zur Selbsthilfe" kannst du auch im Kontext der Situation erklären:* "They help you there to repair your things yourself."

Lehrkraft: What a brilliant idea. Who came up with it?

Du: Er fragt, wer sich das hat einfallen lassen/wer die Idee hatte.

Mitprüfling: *Die Erfinderin war eine Holländerin. Sie hat 2009 das erste Repair Café in Amsterdam eröffnet.*

Du: The inventor was a Dutchwoman/a woman from Holland. She opened the first repair café in Amsterdam in 2009.

✎ *Hinweis: „2009" wird „two thousand nine" ausgesprochen.*

Lehrkraft: I see. What items can people bring?

Du: Welche Dinge kann man (vorbei-/hin-)bringen?

Mitprüfling: *Kaputte Dinge jeglicher Art, die man nicht wegwerfen möchte, wie z. B. kaputte Fahrräder, defekte Handys oder zerbrochenes Spielzeug.*

Du: You can bring broken things of any kind like broken bikes, mobile phones which are out of order/which no longer work or damaged/broken toys.

Lehrkraft: Awesome! What does it cost?

Du: Was kostet es?

Mitprüfling: *Eintritt, Reparaturen und Hilfestellung sind kostenlos, aber Geld- oder Sachspenden sind jederzeit willkommen.*

Du: Admission, repairs and help are free, but you're welcome to/you can donate money or in kind/(other) things.

✎ *Hinweis: Sollte dir das Wort „donate" nicht einfallen, beschreibe, was eine Spende ist:* "give money or objects to someone to help (without taking anything in return/for free)"

Lehrkraft: I see. What is your professional background?

Du: Was ist Ihr beruflicher Hintergrund?

Mitprüfling: *Ich bin ein erfahrener Ingenieur, der seit einem Jahr im Ruhestand ist.*

Du: He is a skilled engineer who's been retired for one year/who stopped working a year ago.

Hinweis: Du kannst „erfahren" auch mit "who has a lot of professional experience" *umschreiben. Die Formulierung „im Ruhestand" lässt sich umschreiben mit* "who stopped working because of his age".

Lehrkraft: Not bad at all. What made you want to work here?

Du: Warum wollten Sie hier arbeiten?

Mitprüfling: *Ich habe Spaß am Reparieren, es kommen hier Jung und Alt miteinander ins Gespräch und Menschen teilen ihr Wissen mit anderen.*

Du: He likes repairing things and the fact that young and old people can meet here to talk and share their knowledge (with each other).

Lehrkraft: That must be a rewarding task. What are the opening hours?

Du: Wie sind die Öffnungszeiten/Wann ist das Repair Café offen?

Mitprüfling: *Das Café ist jeden zweiten Mittwoch im Monat von 13:30 Uhr bis 17:00 Uhr geöffnet.*

Du: The café opens the second Wednesday of every month from half past one in the afternoon until 5 pm.

Lehrkraft: Good to know. My host sister has a broken doll. Maybe we can repair it together.

Du: Seine Gastschwester hat eine kaputte Puppe. Vielleicht können Sie beide sie gemeinsam reparieren.

Filmabend im Planetarium Hamburg

Lehrkraft (= Engländerin): Excuse me, I'd like to know more about the current programmes offered for teenagers.

Du: Entschuldigen Sie, die Dame würde gerne mehr über das aktuelle Programm für Jugendliche/Teenager erfahren.

Mitprüfling (= Dame an der Kasse): *Es gibt verschiedene Vorstellungen je nach Interesse, z. B. einen Film über den Start von „Apollo 11" oder die Dokumentation „Nachtflug durch die Galaxis".*

Du: There are different shows depending on what you're interested in. For example, they're showing a film about the launch/start of "Apollo 11" or the documentary "Nachtflug durch die Galaxis".

Lehrkraft: Ok. So, what exactly is "Apollo 11" about?

Du: Worum genau geht es in „Apollo 11"?

Mitprüfling: *Das ist ein Film über die erste Mondlandung vor über 50 Jahren und den ersten Menschen auf dem Mond. Es ist eine aufgrund modernster 3D-Technik preisgekrönte Produktion.*

Du: It's a movie about the first moon landing more than 50 years ago and the first man on the moon. It's an award-winning production/It won a prize because it was filmed with modern/the latest 3D technology.

Lehrkraft: Cool. And what about the flight through the galaxy?

Du: Und was ist mit „Nachtflug durch die Galaxis"?

Mitprüfling: *Da kann man auf der Reise durch unser Sternensystem erfahren, wie Sterne entstehen und welche es gibt.*

Du: You can learn how stars are formed and which stars exist while going on a journey through our solar system.

Lehrkraft: Not bad. Are those programmes only in German?

Du: Gibt es diese Vorstellungen nur auf Deutsch?

Mitprüfling: *Einige Vorführungen gibt es auf Deutsch, andere auch auf Englisch, Französisch und Spanisch. Entsprechende Termine sind online einsehbar.*

Du: Some shows are in German, some are also in English, French and Spanish. You can check/find/get information on the dates online.

Lehrkraft: Good to know. I will check that. How much are the tickets?

Du: Wieviel kosten die Eintrittskarten?

Mitprüfling: *Die Tickets kosten zwischen 7 € und 12,50 €, abhängig vom Programm und von der Tageszeit. Schüler*innen und Student*innen erhalten einen Rabatt.*

Du: Tickets cost between €7 and €12.50 depending on programme and time. Pupils and students get a discount/pay less/don't have to pay the full price.

Hinweis: „€12.50" wird „12 euros and 50 cents" ausgesprochen.

Lehrkraft: Oh, I see. I only have a credit card. Would that be okay?

Du: Die Dame hat nur eine Kreditkarte. Ist das in Ordnung/Geht das?

Mitprüfling: *An der Kasse gibt es nur Barzahlung, übers Internet ist die Zahlung auch mit Kreditkarte möglich.*

Du: Here you can only pay cash, but if you book online you can also pay by credit card.

Hinweis: Da du dich laut der gegebenen Situation an der Kasse befindest, kannst du deine Übersetzung mit „Here" beginnen und musst gar nicht überlegen, was „an der Kasse" auf Englisch heißt.

Lehrkraft: Alright. What else should I know?

Du: **Was sollte sie noch wissen?**

Mitprüfling: *Die Website gibt es auch auf Englisch zum Nachlesen.*

Du: **The website is also available in English if you want to read the information again.**

Lehrkraft: Harhar, good to know. Thank you so much for your help.

Du: **Das ist gut zu wissen. Vielen Dank für Ihre Hilfe.**

Um dir die Lösungen zur Prüfung 2023 schnellstmöglich zur Verfügung stellen zu können, bringen wir sie in digitaler Form heraus.

Sobald die Original-Prüfungsaufgaben 2023 freigegeben sind, können die dazugehörigen Lösungen als PDF auf der Plattform **MyStark** heruntergeladen werden (Zugangscode vgl. Umschlaginnenseite vorne im Buch).

Aktuelle Prüfung

www.stark-verlag.de/mystark